I0653568

LET THE WILD OUT

MADELYN PORTER
MICHELLE M. PILLOW

THE RAVEN BOOKS LLC

FROM THE AUTHOR

This is fantasy. In real life always practice safe sex.

ABOUT LET THE WILD OUT

PARANORMAL SHAPESHIFTER EROTIC MÉNAGE ROMANCE

Rachel Dunne thinks she's safe from the politics of her people by keeping a low profile in America. When she comes face to face with one of the clan chiefs in search of a mate, she's stunned yet is undeniably attracted. There is a catch—law states one queen to two opposing clan chiefs. It's hard enough fighting off the advances of one alpha king, can she possibly resist two?

To my BFF's alter ego, Rory Michaels. I guess that would make me your BFF, or, um, my alter ego's BFF is your alter ego, or are we the alter egos, or I'm your alter ego's BFF and you're my alter ego's…damn. Who are we again?

ONE

EVERYONE SHOULD HAVE *AT LEAST* TWO LOVERS.

That's what Rachel Dunne's crazy aunt used to tell her anyway. Her mother would have rolled over in her grave if she'd known her father's sister had been given custody. After her parents died, Aunt Elvie was the only family member who could take her in. Rachel spent her teenage years under the care of a free lovin', spirit séance havin', illegal herb growin', occasionally under arrest, Auntie Elvie. Luckily the sheriff was one of Elvie's pot customer slash on-and-off-again lovers, and Elvie never stayed behind bars for too long.

It wasn't an ideal childhood. But what Elvie lacked in modern morals and conventions she more than made up with love and patience. As for an Uncle Elvie, there wasn't one—there were several. Elvie rotated her lovers like most people changed toothbrushes, and she always kept at least two of them around at a time. Though, for their kind, such things were not unusual.

Oh, Aunt Elvie also happened to be a bird shifter. Rachel always thought it accounted for her flighty behavior and great appetite for life. Though, how a bird shifter could get arrested in the middle of a forest was beyond her. Rachel suspected her aunt liked being put in cuffs.

For some reason, Aunt Elvie and her childhood had been on her mind a lot lately.

"What kind are you?"

Rachel pretended not to hear the man who spoke, keeping her attention on the ebook reader she held. She had seen him following her as she left the bookstore where guest authors, Mandy M. Roth and Michelle M. Pillow, had joint book readings. She'd felt his presence as she walked the streets and smelled him as he came into the coffee shop. She didn't need to look at him to know he had dark hair and a rock-solid body. That much she'd seen from the reflection in the bookstore window. But experience taught her to stay away from other shifters. They had a wildness about them, an animalistic quality and a freedom Rachel fought hard to control in herself.

"What kind are you?" The unmistakable

brogue of his Gaelic accent seemed out of place in the small Colorado town. That might account for his forward behavior. The shifters she'd met from overseas tended to have less puritanical ways. In America, unless on a preserve, shifters tended to mind their own business.

Rachel glanced at the hand he pressed flat against the table. There was no point in denying his claim. She could smell the shifter on him, as he could on her. However, his fragrance was potent and raw. He'd changed recently and, if the prickling sense of danger curling through her was any indication, he was dangerous. No wild bird here. Without looking up, she said, "I heard you the first two times, but my parents told me to never talk to strangers. Just keep it moving, buddy. I'm not in the life and I'm not looking for friends."

The man turned his hand over so she could see his palm. An ancient, circular design had been burned into the flesh with a branding iron. It looked old, probably given to him in childhood in an ancient ritual. She stiffened, not needing further introduction. Rachel didn't move for a long moment. She knew that mark. Everyone with shifter blood knew that mark. She'd never expected to see it in her lifetime, had hoped not. As far as she'd known, the marked ones were all living overseas, and she preferred it that way.

Slowly lifting the back of her hand to her head in a subtle gesture of respect Aunt Elvie had taught her, she said, "My chief."

"For someone not in the life, you know who I am." He pulled his fingers into a fist. "Now I asked you a question. What kind are you?"

"Trout," Rachel lied, finally looking up at him. "My kind is a trout. I'm diluted blood."

She wasn't sure it was wise to lie to her clan chief, but if he was asking about her kind, then being a tame creature of the river wasn't useful to anyone. It had been a long time since she shifted, so her smell wouldn't be potent at all. The lie would be believable. Hopefully he'd leave her alone now. Rachel fought the nervousness in her stomach. If he caught her lying to him she wasn't sure what he'd do. The stories from the old country were brutal, practically medieval.

He slid into the chair across from her. "Trout?"

"Yes, my chief. A fish. When I change I swim in streams and try not to get hooked by fishermen while avoiding other spawning creatures. You can see why I'm not interested in the life." Rachel made a move to stand, refusing to look into his eyes in case he sensed her fear. "If you would excuse me, I have to get to—"

"Wait." He reached for her hand. The warmth of his touch took her by surprise.

"Yes?" Was it just her imagination, or could she feel the scar on his palm? Her attention focused on it, on him. Awareness shot through her.

"Who are your family? Which clan?"

"My family is gone. My aunt, Elvie Dunne, raised me. She passed two years back. My father, her brother, belonged to yours, the Duncanis clan. I don't talk to any others. Any other questions you have are better directed at someone else. I hear there are shifters living in Colorado Springs. Perhaps you should try there." Rachel withdrew her hand and he let her go. "Excuse me, Chief, but I can't lose my job."

"No reason to be so formal. Call me Douglas."

She nodded, not saying his name or meeting his eyes. Grabbing her ebook reader, she held it a little too tightly.

As she walked away, she detected his whisper, "I'll be seeing you, little trout."

Rachel really hoped not.

TWO

Douglas absently scratched at his scar as he watched the petite brunette leave the coffee shop. A fish? She couldn't be the shifter he searched for. As chief of one of the two shifter clans, he needed a powerful woman, a woman whose shifter blood was strong; a woman the other clan chief would respect and also be willing to take as a bride. Since the Medieval clan battles, that was their way. One bride to the two male chiefs.

As chieftess queen, his future bride would act as an intermediary between the two clans, and none would know which father sired her children, though occasionally the lineage could be guessed at merely by looking at the offspring. The oldest child would go to the oldest chief, the second to the youngest, and the third to the oldest chief again, continuing back and forth for however many offspring there were, to be raised according to the father clan's traditions. For this reason, royalty never married royalty, instead choosing a bride who showed signs of strong shifter blood.

A fish? Too bad.

Douglas had grown up with these facts of his birthright and accepted his destiny. After forty years as an unmarried chief, his people were restless for new royal blood. When the chiefs didn't have children, his people had a tendency to panic. Without leadership, the old battles could be resumed and chaos would ensue. Thousands had been lost in those dark times.

Chief William of the Cononious Clan had just ascended to his rule after his adopted father, the former chief, Tobias died. The people had been pushing them both for a bride. In truth, he did not know William well. The man was not Douglas's blood brother. They had not been raised together and only met every other year at clan rituals. Now they would be sharing a wife.

With his father newly in the grave, William didn't have time for the search. It didn't matter. Douglas and William both knew what to look for. The bride had to be strong, full-blooded and, though hardly an official requirement, young and pretty. Though, "young" to a shifter was much different than young to a human. A shifter's life-span was three times as long as any so-called mortal.

It was too bad. The little trout shifter was pretty. She would have definitely been a candidate if not for her diluted blood. Though some shifters still cared about such things, his decision was more practical. With diluted blood, she'd not live as long as he did, and she would potentially give the chiefs less children. Since Douglas's own mother had given birth to only one child, leaving Tobias to adopt William, the people were anxious to replenish the royal lines.

Still, the panther inside of him was interested. If not a wife, then a lover while he looked for a bride. After he married, there would be no more lovers. It was their way.

Feeling his pocket vibrate, Douglas took out his phone. William had texted him about the picture he'd snapped of the pretty brunette. "Who is she? She is very beautiful."

Sighing, Douglas answered, "Not who I thought she was. Just a pretty woman."

He closed his phone. A waiter appeared carrying food. "You going to pay for the lady's sandwich?"

Douglas glanced to where the woman had

disappeared and smiled. "Can I get that to go? She had to leave suddenly."

The waiter nodded and disappeared. Douglas took out his wallet. He smiled. Part of him was very happy at the idea of not having to share this woman.

THREE

ENGLAND

William deleted the text from Douglas and again brought up the picture of the brunette woman. When he'd first seen her, his body had lurched in interest. It was the first positive feeling he'd had since the death of his adopted father. Douglas's mother had died giving birth to her only son and neither of the old chieftains wanted another mate after that. The Duncanis chief had his male heir in Douglas, so the Cononious chief had adopted the orphaned William as his own.

In truth, he didn't know Douglas, at least not beyond his reputation. Where William was studious, it was said Douglas was reckless. It might have been due to the fact William shifted into wolf, a form known for its inherently wild temperament. He had to fight for control against his natural urges if he was to be a leader.

Douglas was a panther, a refined animal until cornered, which could partially account for the chief's lack of control as a man. He didn't have to try very hard to fight the beast within. He'd also been born into royalty and his shifter subjects didn't watch his every move as closely. Douglas's uncontrolled appetites as a man worried William when it came to choosing their bride. He'd probably pick someone just as untamed. Luckily, though, William would have final say in whomever Douglas wanted.

Hearing footsteps, he closed his phone and looked towards the end of the courtyard. The English weather was unseasonably cool, but he found he didn't mind it. Outside, the world seemed quiet and still. It was inside the English manor house that seemed full of chaos and demands.

William always wondered if the fact he wasn't born into the life of royalty made it harder for him. Douglas always seemed at ease with his role. William often felt like an imposter.

"I thought I'd find you out here," Magda said. The old maid had been with the family for over two hundred years. She'd been his caretaker when he was younger, always following him, always whispering duty in his ear until his thoughts were incessantly filled with what he must do and how he must act. He knew that look on her face well. She wanted him inside with his guests.

Before she could speak, he preemptively stopped her. "I was answering a message from Douglas in America and needed the quiet. It was about a potential bride."

Her expression instantly changed. She wasn't excited, not really, not as he imagined most people were when talking about a wedding, but she seemed pleased that he was thinking about marriage in general. She nodded, all censure fading from her features. "When you're finished, we need to go over the preparations for tonight. The vampire king will be here at dusk."

Unable to help himself, he said, "Be sure to hang wreathes of garlic on the window."

"Boy," she warned, even as she tried not to smile. It was no secret that Magda hated vampires. She thought of them as lower beings, even lower than humans. The woman was a shifter elitist.

Then, on impulse, he said, "Douglas needs me in America to look at candidates."

"Why doesn't he bring them here?" Magda asked, clearly not seeing the wisdom. "Or, better yet, find a bride here."

"We're trying to be discreet," William said.

"It's been agreed between the two of us that we should find a bride from America for there are too many politics at play here. However, we cannot risk angering the old European families. So, if I am there to meet with the other chief to oversee the conditions of our American brothers, no one will question it if we happen to find our wife amongst the Americans."

"A heathen bride." Magda shook her head. "Let me see who he has in mind for you, boy."

William opened his phone and brought up the picture of the brunette. "Here's one he's seriously considering." There was no reason to mention she wasn't suitable.

Magda eyed her. "She's very skinny. What kind is she?"

"I'm not sure. Douglas won't say over the phone in case others watch what we're doing. That is why I must go to Colorado."

"What about Lisbetha? She's very pretty and from an old family. Or, if you prefer someone less meek, how about Faith or her younger sisters, Hope and Charity? They are all very pretty girls and their father is well respected." Magda had offered each girl before. "If you want wild, then choose Ginger. Dark, take Judith. Blonde, Lisbetha again."

As if bidden by their names, Lisbetha and

Ginger appeared in the distance. Lisbetha smiled and lifted her fingers to greet him. Ginger leaned into the other woman, lifting her hand to cover a whisper before giggling. Without waiting to be summoned into his presence, the young ladies walked towards him. They batted their lashes and dipped their chins in a practiced effort to get his attention. Threads of silver filtered through their eyes. All he had to do was say one word and they would follow him anywhere, let him do anything. If such a thing wouldn't complicate his life in the extreme, he'd have taken either of them to bed to find release.

"My chief," Lisbetha breathed. Her blonde hair curled around her face, each lock pristine and purposefully placed. He'd never seen her shifted, but he was told she was a rare bird called an Asian-crested ibis, which made her incredibly special. Though hardly powerful in the sense of physical strength, rare animals were prized.

"*Mm—my* chief," Ginger said, the low tone full of invitation. She was bolder than the others, often running through the forest when she knew he was there, rubbing her kitten scent on the trees, walking naked in human form, breasts pushed out and lips pursed. Seeing his attention on her mouth, she licked her bottom lip.

"Ladies," came his obligatory answer.

"Mistress," they said in unison to Magda.

Magda paused a few seconds too long, as if waiting for William to strike up a conversation. When he didn't, she urged, "Would you two be so kind as to see to the hall? We need to ensure the servants did not put out the real silver."

"Of course," Lisbetha said, eager to please. Ginger pretended to pout but let her friend lead her away.

"You could have given them some encouragement," Magda scolded.

"Why? To do so would be cruel. They would be better off setting their sights on another." William eyed his phone, thinking of the woman Douglas found. "Douglas would never consent to them."

"Very well. If there is no stopping you, I will pack our bags." Magda turned to leave.

"No. I wish for you to stay here." William stood and placed his hand on her arm. He took his phone back from her. "I'll trust you to keep me informed of all that happens in my absence. I need someone I can trust to see to things. You, better than anyone, knows what must be done."

"Yes, my chief." She nodded once, a curt, disapproving gesture, and turned to go.

FOUR

Rachel ignored the burning in her lungs as she ran through the woods. The nature trail was long and isolated, just as she liked it. Running full speed was as close to the freedom of shifting as she could get. Most people stayed to the well-worn paths, but she preferred to be alone, and there was no better place than on the land Aunt Elvie left her. She liked to visit the old house in the woods at least once a month. Along with it, Elvie had left her enough money to live on. Rachel still worked though, training wait staff and keeping the accounts at a sports bar and grill. It wasn't glamorous, but it was work and gave her the freedom to make her own schedule. Plus, if she was at work, she didn't have to go through the depressing chore of cooking for one.

The steady beat of her feet on the ground echoed off the trees. She listened to the sounds of the forest, able to hear the distant birds and insects as if they were right beside her. Small animals roamed the surrounding woods—rabbit thirty paces to the north, squirrel running up a tree fifty paces to the northeast. Narrowing her eyes, she looked ahead, focusing on the distance. She knew if any looked at her, her normally green gaze would be filled with liquid silver. The power of the shift was seductive and strong. It was only with years of control that she managed to keep those things within her at bay. But here, in the forest during her secret runs, she was free.

She detected a new smell in the forest and slowed her pace by a fraction. That's when she noticed another set of footsteps. Whoever it was had been keeping a perfect rhythm with her to hide an approach. A few seconds later, the other person's step slowed to match hers. It was too late. She'd heard it. She was being followed.

The home she'd inherited was ten miles away. She could tell by the smell of overgrown marijuana fields on the wind. Luckily for Rachel, she knew this land. Excitement pumped in her veins. Let the other runner chase her. He'd never be able to catch up to her speed. She quickened her pace, moving as fast as she possibly could on two legs. Her heart pounded. The rhythm behind her doubled. Whoever it was ran faster. Excitement turned to concern. The person gained on her position.

Her heart felt as if it might explode and her skin tingled. She could feel her body urging her to shift. Rachel tried to fight it, but the compulsion was too strong. She ripped out of her T-shirt, throwing it aside. Her bone snapped and she almost cried out in pain. Her body flew forward, palms hitting the ground. Unable to stop now if she wanted to, she raced on all fours. Her clothing fell behind her, forgotten on the path. Paws replaced hands and feet. Fur of the wolf replaced flesh. The last to change was her face, her nose and mouth elongating with awful snaps of her delicate bones. No matter how many times she'd lived through it, the pain was unimaginable yet thankfully brief.

Her motions became a stream of instinct. She turned from the path, running into the dense forest. Raw, natural urges filled her—the urge to run, the urge to feed, the urge for sex and sleep and shelter and survival. But more potent than any of those things was the need for freedom.

She leapt over a log. Whatever was behind her

followed her deeper into the trees. The creature was fast, gaining on her with each second. She felt more than saw her pursuer jump out from behind a pine. Paws brushed over her back, barely missing her.

She didn't have a choice. Rachel turned to fight, snarling to frighten off whoever charged her. A large, grey, male wolf faced her. Another wolf shifter? Here? In her forest? She edged away from him, her feet stamping on the ground. He didn't advance, but instead studied her as if curious. She sniffed the air, not recognizing his scent.

Neither of them moved towards the other. Their sides rose and fell, matching in rhythm. She studied his blue eyes flecked with silver. They made her nervous. His body quivered and he began to shift. What was he doing? She glanced around the forest, about ready to run. Fur grew into flesh. Muscles stretched. Before she could react, a naked man crouched before her. Her breathing deepened.

The blue eyes looked the same, penetrating and a little dangerous. Shadows fell across his blond hair and strong face. Broad shoulders, thick arms, big chest, tapered waist… She shivered.

Rachel had never been so glad to be in shifted form in her life. Her brain could comprehend what she was seeing, but her body didn't react. He kept his fingertips pressed into the leaf-covered floor. As if expecting her to transform for him, he nodded at her.

She couldn't shift, not now. She'd be naked. He'd be naked. They'd be naked together. She didn't know who he was, what he wanted, why he chased her. And, unless she shifted, she couldn't ask him.

He leaned forward, pressing a knee into the ground so he could reach out to touch her. "Who are you?"

The sound of his deep voice prodded her into action. She took off running and didn't stop until she reached her aunt's house. Shifting on the back porch, she grabbed the hidden key and locked herself inside.

❧

WILLIAM GRINNED AS HE WATCHED THE FEMALE wolf shifter run away. The predator in him wanted to chase her down, but he'd already done that and she'd refused to reveal herself. Okay, so in truth, he wanted to do much more than chase her down. Jogging through the dense forest, he found his cellular phone clipped to his cotton shorts. He flipped it open and dialed. "Hey, Douglas, it's me. I've got a strong prospect. How soon can you get to the forest sanctuary? We have some hunting to do."

❧

RACHEL HUDDLED NAKED IN ELVIE'S CABIN FOR nearly twenty minutes, listening to the forest outside, before finally trusting it was safe to move about. The home was decorated like any self-respecting hunting lodge, minus the animal carcasses hanging above the mantel. Dark browns, reds and forest greens offset the medium brown of the log walls. The cabin had everything a person might need—a generator and well, guns and knives, food stuffs and furnishings, more liquor than twenty shifters could drink in a lifetime. Rachel suspected there had been a moonshine still on the land at one time.

Narrowing her eyes, she scanned the surrounding landscape from the doorway before hurrying to the generator to turn it on. Shifters would avoid an occupied house in the forest for fear of hunters, and in their unshifted forms she'd just be another hard-ass homemaker with a rifle. So long as she didn't let them get too close, other shifters wouldn't detect her recent transformation.

Once the generator was running, she went back inside, locked the doors and took down a rifle from over the mantel place to make sure it was loaded. Since she was already naked and incredibly dirty from her run through the woods, she hopped into the shower. The generator hadn't been on for long, and the well water was still freezing cold. She didn't linger.

Is that you, baby? Rachel smiled at the memory of her aunt's voice. She could still hear the exact tone of it. *When did you get home?*

"Long before you flew your way into bed, Elv," Rachel whispered to her reflection in the mirror. Then, breathing deeply, she imagined she could still smell her aunt's perfume.

That is a shame, baby. You should be in the forest having fun. Let the wild out. It is in your blood.

Rachel brushed her hair and made her way to her old room to find something to wear. Then, falling onto the bed that had cradled so much of her teenage angst, she sighed heavily. Her thoughts turned to the shifter in the woods. A wolf. She'd never met another wolf shifter. In fact, she'd been sure she was one of the very few living in the Unites States. Most of the "power animals", as they were called, migrated to the homeland for they were valued for their strong shifter genetics and were treated like kings in the old country. For all her aunt's guidance in taking multiple lovers, letting the wild out, and the benefits of sleeping with the local law enforcement in exchange for favors, Elvie had given Rachel one piece of very valuable advice—hide the wolf from the others. If they knew, they'd take her to the European court where she would be encouraged none-too-gently to mate with another powerful shifter.

But more than a wolf, the male shifter was a handsome man. Her breathing deepened. Perhaps her suppressed wild had finally grown tired of being chained up. The recent shift didn't help. First, there was the chief who followed her to the coffee shop the week before. Okay, so she'd barely looked him in the face, but she remembered those strong hands, tapering fingers. In her fantasies, she could be with him in a way her reality would never permit. She hadn't been back to that part of town since. In fact, it's why she found herself in the forest. She was hiding out until she was sure he'd moved on. Now there was the wolf man— naked and primal, everything a royal chief was not. Had she shifted into human before the wolf man, she had no doubt he would have lunged for her.

Her stomach tightened. Thoughts of being taken on her hands and knees pranced through her brain. The forest had been both open and isolated at the same time. Wolf man's naked state left nothing to the imagination, from his strong limbs to his thick chest to his unmistakable arousal. There was no doubt what kind of lover he'd be. In fact, she'd bet he'd take her so hard she'd end up howling in pleasure. The shifter in her grinned wickedly at the thought. The human in her wasn't so sure. The few lovers she had in her life were never other shifters.

And what about the Duncanis chief? She heard tales of his prowess, mostly from Elvie who talked about their leader like he was some rock star. Elvie said he shifted into the form of a black panther. Apparently, he was graceful in bed, enjoying the chase and first conquest before moving on. Whereas the wolf man would take a woman on the forest floor like a beast, the chief would be the kind of guy who would prefer a lush penthouse and silken sheets. Both fantasies held great appeal.

The longing she felt caused her to hit her stomach in an effort to stop it. She pushed her thighs closely together, trying to will the sensations away. It didn't work. If anything, the sensations became worse until every subtle movement felt like a caress. How could she resist two prime fantasies?

Rachel squirmed on the bed. Her breathing

deepened. Images of a silken penthouse flipped back and forth with the image of the forest. Before she realized what she was doing, her hands were on her breasts, massaging them. Her hand dipped down, inching lower across her stomach.

FIVE

WILLIAM FELT AS IF HIS INSIDES WERE SET ON fire. He was already aroused from the chase, and the strange sexual energy surrounding the isolated, lodge-style cabin in the woods didn't help him control the animal instincts. He stepped from the forest, completely dressed in his previously discarded clothes—knee-length shorts, a T-shirt, and running shoes.

Though some of the outside plants were overgrown, the home had a wild beauty to it. Looking at the surrounding view, he could see the appeal, especially for his kind. Well traveled paths encircled the place, leading off to the generator shed and other outbuildings. It was the soft sound of the running generator that drew his attention to the home's location.

Closing his eyes, he breathed deeply. His flesh tingled. This was a place of power, probably made so by generations of shifters living on the land, working the old natural magic—protection spells and the harnessing of primal sexual energy. The protection spells kept him from determining exactly where the other wolf had run off to.

On the doorframe, old carvings marked the place as a sanctuary. It wasn't surprising, considering his old maps marked the entire mountain as shifter safe. Without hesitation, he knocked loudly and focused his hearing.

A faint gasp was followed by the sound of something falling. He turned his attention up to the second level. Somewhere above, a woman whispered, "Ah shit, what the—? Ow, damn it." Another thud sounded.

William chuckled. Seconds later, footsteps were running down stairs. By the time the door opened, he was grinning, truly curious as to what would be on the other side.

Flush-cheeked and out of breath stood the woman whose picture Douglas had sent to him. Her hair looked as if it had been wet, only to curl around her temples as it dried. Wide, green eyes studied him, more stunned than welcoming. She didn't move to let him in.

"Sanctuary," he said, though it was clear he

wasn't running from anyone. He shifted his weight to the side.

"What?" She furrowed her brows. She had the cutest American accent. So very puritanical.

"Sanctuary." This time he pointed at the doorframe.

The woman blinked slowly and then leaned out of the door to look at where he indicated. "Is that what that means? My aunt said it meant…" She made a weak noise, her cheeks coloring. "Never mind. How can I help you?"

"You can start by inviting me in for the night."

"Excuse me?" She began to reach for the door, clearly intent on slamming it shut. He slid his foot forward, blocking it. She lifted her hand to her side, revealing a rifle as she pulled the barrel in front of her.

"I take it your aunt hasn't told you about shifter law."

"Shifter?" The woman arched a brow, pretending not to understand him.

He chuckled. "I smell a recent shift on you." When the body morphed, there was a subtle universal scent that lingered to help shifters recognize each other. When she didn't point the gun directly at him, he leaned closer. "That's not all I smell on you."

Her breathing visibly deepened.

"I didn't interrupt anything, did I?" William inhaled deeply, letting his eyes shift with silver. His tone lowered, as the beast inside of him grew interested. Her flesh was clean, scented with a floral soap, but he detected the subtle fragrance of sexual awareness. At his nearness, the scent grew, as if inviting him in. His cock, already aching, nearly pulsed with need.

"N-no," she stammered.

William lifted his hand to the carved door-frame, caressing it slowly. "This means this home is sanctuary to all shifters who would ask for it. You cannot deny me," his eyes moved down over her body, "entrance."

Her fingers loosened on the gun and he reached to take it from her. His eyes stayed fixed on her. He set the gun aside and stepped into the home. It had been a long time since he'd taken a woman, since before his ascension. Now, too many eyes were on him, wanting something from him, watching him. This woman didn't know who he was. He found her lack of knowledge aroused him more. The pheromones were powerful between them. How could she resist them? How could he?

He listened to the house. They were alone. He let a smile creep over his features. "Was that you in the woods?"

"Woods?" she asked before shaking her head in denial.

Pity, he thought. He would have liked to meet the wolf woman. *Oh well, you will do, pretty one.*

"There are people..." She made a move to gesture behind her.

"No. There is no one." He lowered his jaw. The sweet smell of her body let him know she was wet. The predator in him liked the game she played.

"There will be," she insisted. He let her have the lie. "So, you see, there are no extra rooms. However, there's a town about fifteen miles west of here. You look well enough to jog the distance."

He reached for her, touching her hair. "I'll stay in your room."

"Oh?" she breathed.

He wasn't sure if the look she gave him was interest or embarrassment. William could only assume it was interest. He'd never met a shifter embarrassed about sex. "I smell you."

"I showered." Her chest rose and fell.

"I smell your wet sex."

"I...ah, shower—um." She blinked, glancing back and forth as if she might run. "I mean, I...you...no."

"I, you, no?" He licked his lips. The sound of her breath punctuated each second. "I, you, yes."

"Yes?" Her lids fell lazily over her eyes and she leaned into him, as if finally giving in to her desires. She breathed in his scent, her shoulders lifting.

"Oh yes." He nodded in agreement.

William slipped his hand behind her head to hold her in place as he leaned over to kiss her. She didn't instantly attack him, but instead let her lips part as if she was unsure what to do. He took the hesitant invitation by letting his tongue glide between her lips, forcing them to open wider. Light moans escaped her, but William knew how to kiss a woman into complete submission, and soon she was moving against him. He drew his tongue into her mouth, rubbing it gently. Their bodies were drawn towards each other, as if by an unstoppable force.

Soft breasts pressed into his chest. He ran his hands down her back to cup her ass. Massaging hard, he pulled her flush to his cock. The second he rubbed his erection against her, she let loose a small gasp of surprise. The woman pulled at his clothes, forcing him to be rid of his shirt. She drew her mouth to his neck, biting and kissing him as she explored his chest with her hands. She seemed fascinated by the muscles, eagerly tracing each one.

William growled. He ripped at her clothing,

letting his nails sharpen into claws so he could tear through the material. A lacy, pink bra cupped her breasts. He groaned, seeing it beneath the wisps of torn fabric.

Letting go of her, he pushed the shorts from his hips. The woman stepped back, blinking hard. She stared at his cock and slowly lifted her hand as if to keep him away. "I can't…we shouldn't."

"You were doing just fine," he assured her. William wasn't sure how he'd stop himself, but he would if she commanded it. He kept his movements slow as he inched closer. If she ran away, the animal in him would want to chase. "Let us find pleasure."

"I…but…" She again glanced down at his erection.

He refused to take himself in hand as she stared. Instead, he pushed his hips forward so his arousal jutted towards her. "Feel me. Then decide if you want me inside you."

She turned her hand, reaching for him. He smiled. Her finger pushed to the tip of his cock, and his whole body shivered in response.

"Ah, you are a magnificent tease," he groaned, closing his eyes. "If you tell me to stop, I will stop." He again opened them as her hand slid more fully onto his shaft. "Don't tell me to stop."

To his disappointment, she didn't speak. He

wanted to hear her say she wanted him. What man wouldn't like to hear such a thing from a beautiful woman? Instead, she was silent but for the gentle rise and fall of her soft breathing.

The silver light in her eyes caught his attention, saying more than words ever could. He jerked her near. There was no more hesitation. The primal beasts inside them took over. She dug her nails into his shoulders and neck. He grabbed hold of her hips, lifting her off the floor. Standing in the middle of the room, he held her against him. Her legs wrapped his waist. He could have taken her there, like that, but he wanted leverage.

William backed her against the wall, pressing her into the thick, wood logs. The smell of her flesh drove him wild. Nails scratched almost painfully into his arms. He felt his gums tighten as his teeth extended down. He wanted to bite her, devour her, sink his body into hers. The need was too great, too carnal and out of control. He positioned his shaft along her sex, drawn forward by the moisture guarding her pussy.

Mindlessly, he thrust, crying out as her tight flesh enveloped him completely. For the first time in a long time he felt free. No eyes were on him, watching the new chief. She didn't know who he was. She was with him because she desired him, no other reason. Their bodies strained. He leaned over, taking a ripe breast into his mouth. Sucking the erect nipple, he moaned. His hips flexed, beginning the natural rhythm of pleasure—out, in, out, in, release, contract, push, pull.

He could easily hear the sounds of the forest, but all of his attention focused on his erection and the sweet, wet glide of entering her tight pussy. She made a weak noise and hit his arm. William realized his mouth had slipped to her shoulder and he'd bitten down a little too hard in his excitement. Three tiny dots and a single trail of blood marred her tanned flesh. Without even thinking about it, he licked the wound.

The wolf howled inside of him. Had this woman been human, he would have never been able to let the animal out to play. He didn't need a mirror to know his eyes were filled with silver, his teeth were elongated fangs, and his fingernails had sharpened into deadly weapons.

Silver filled her eyes, showing the only hint of her true nature. Brunette hair fell around her face in disarray. Her full lips parted and he stared at them. She came hard. Her upper back pressed into the wall as she arched into him. Her body trembled, calling to his. He thrust hard, finding release in her sweet depths.

❧

Douglas breathed deeply, torn between hard, blood-pumping arousal and deep jealousy. His woman, the one he'd found, his little fish, his soon-to-be last lover before he married, was being taken against the wall of the isolated sanctuary home. He had followed William's scent to the cabin, not that it had been hard with all the shifter signs leading the way. Some of the markings were old, but he could still smell them.

Douglas never expected this—William taking the woman he wanted. Even jealousy could not stop the arousal he felt as he watched the two of them, kind of the same arousal he felt when watching porn or live sex shows. Like most high-level males, William was in great shape. His ass flexed, showing the force with which he pumped into her. Douglas wished he'd move to the side so he could see more than the woman's legs bouncing up and down behind the man's back.

Douglas knew he wasn't supposed to be jealous of the other chief. They would be sharing a bride, after all, but he couldn't help it. He'd been fantasizing about his brunette beauty since the coffee shop the week before. He had even searched for her, but she never showed herself, and the coffee shop and bookstore owners didn't know who she was. The most they said was that she kept to herself and paid cash.

William lowered her to the ground and she swayed. Douglas ducked from his place by the window. He'd seen more than enough. Glancing down, he realized his hand was down the front of his charcoal slacks and he gripped his erection. He hurried from the porch as stealthily as he could move, not wanting to get caught with his hand down his pants.

Once behind the generator building, he made quick work of his jealous desires. He drew his arousal out of the fly of his slacks without taking them down and pumped his fist over the length. The image of William fucking the woman was burned into his mind. He wanted to be the one pressing her into the wall. He wanted to be the one stretching her pussy to fit his shaft. He wanted to be the one inside the cabin. Cursed wolf! He was the one who'd found her. If not for him, William wouldn't have known of her existence.

He came, but it was a bittersweet release. Leaning against the shed, he scanned the surrounding forest. First, he would catch his breath while waiting for the two lovebirds in the cabin to finish up. Then he would act as if he hadn't seen a damn thing.

SIX

"WHAT ARE YOU THINKING? YOU JUST ARRIVED here in America. This is the woman I told you about. I've been looking for her. I told you I wanted her as a lover, and yet I come here to find you rutting like a dog in heat." Douglas glared in irritation, the fire of the shift in his eyes. He wanted to punch the other chief, even as every logical reason why he shouldn't filtered through his brain. He balled his hand into a fist, making a physical effort to hold himself back.

"To lay claim, the woman must be willing. She was willing with me," William answered calmly. Then, as if unable to help himself, he said, "And I wasn't the only rutting dog."

Douglas's frown deepened. He glanced to where the woman had disappeared into the kitchen. Apparently Elvie had never bothered to explain the list of sanctuary duties to her niece. Rachel didn't even question their claim to stay, though it became clear in all of two seconds that she didn't want either of them inside her home.

"She's hardly a dog," Douglas whispered.

"What then? You never did tell me."

"She said fish," Douglas answered. "Trout."

William's smile faded somewhat. Douglas nodded in confirmation. He could understand the man's disappointment. The council of elders would never accept a water shifter as their queen.

"Then I claim her as my lover," William said. "She has already shown she favors me."

"She might have slept with you," Douglas said, "but she did not declare her intent to be your lover only. She might decide otherwise. Besides, I said I claimed her first. I have as much right as you do. I said the words first. You claimed her body first. I think we're both within our rights."

"What are you saying?" William's entire being stiffened, and the threat of the shift entered his eyes. The man didn't look like he wanted to share. Well, that was too damned bad. Douglas had wanted the woman first, had found her. It wasn't like he wanted to share her with William.

Douglas frowned. Canine shifters were always so hot-blooded and quick to argue. Felines were much more relaxed and calculating. He ignored the fact that he'd been ready to pounce on the werewolf a few seconds before. The fact was William had already been with the woman. There was no denying it or taking it back. "We have to learn to share eventually."

William took a deep breath. Douglas could see the idea did not sit well with the wolf man. After some thought, William said, "That is different. That will be our wife. We both know the reasons for such an arrangement and it is our duty to agree. But this—"

"And you think those arguments will make it easier?" Douglas countered. "You speak of the woman who will bear our children and unite our clans. Can you not tell me that if the first child looks like you, and is living with me as my son, you won't feel the urge to fight? Or when our wife comes to my bed, you will not want to storm my castle and retrieve her? If we pick someone we can care about, we will have to deal with our urges to mark her as our sole territory. If we pick someone we don't care for, we'll have to live with the unsatisfying arrangement for the sake of duty. I don't know about you, but I would rather share a woman I cared for than live with an empty heart and cold bed, begetting heirs in a loveless marriage."

William considered that for a long moment and then slowly nodded. "You are right, of course. We must learn to share that which we desire most."

"I do not like it either," Douglas said. "But it is a sacrifice we must make for the sake of the clans. Our wife will be the linchpin that unites us all. If the shifter clans fight, we will be weakened to outside forces. We will be exposed to humans. Vampires will make a power play."

"The vampires visited my home before I left," William said. "They were testing me to see my resolve."

"Those creatures always test their boundaries. They do not think Southern and Western Europe is enough territory." Douglas frowned. He really disliked dealing with vampires. Something about their pale flesh and red eyes left him unsettled. "We do not have to like the arrangement of our marriage."

"But we are agreed," William stated. "We must learn to share. So long as the woman is willing to be with you, we will not fight over her."

"We are agreed." Douglas nodded. He heard Rachel coming towards them.

William lowered his voice. "Then I will not stand in your way. According to custom, it is your turn to take her to bed. I would wish you luck, but…" The wolf man shrugged.

"I do not need luck," Douglas answered, feeling the anticipation of seduction welling within him.

SEVEN

Rachel paused, trying to keep her hands from shaking as she held the tray before her. As much as she tried to tell herself that the Duncanis chief didn't know what she and William had done, she knew it was a lie. Even she could smell the sex lingering in the room the two men now sat in. That's what sucked about being around shifters. It was hard to keep such things a secret.

More mortifying than that, Rachel couldn't believe what she'd done. She'd had sex with a stranger like some sort of out-of-control animal. Name introductions hadn't even come until after, when Chief Douglas stood in her doorway claiming sanctuary. Who was she to turn away a chief? She wanted to keep a low profile in the shifter community. Incurring the wrath of a chief wasn't the way to do that. Maybe they'd only stay one night and then leave. A girl could hope.

Sanctuary. Technically, she had inherited the land and the home, but Rachel was now coming to realize that her aunt left out some key elements in her will. She should have paid more attention to what Elvie was doing instead of just assuming the revolving door was part of her aunt's hippie ways. Clearly Elvie's life wasn't all pot plants and orgies.

Her hands shook. The tray of drinks felt heavy, and she gripped it tighter to keep from dropping it on the floor. Ice tinkled as she stepped into the living room. The two men automatically stood from the couch as she entered. She hesitated at the attention. "I'm afraid the house isn't very well stocked. I mean, there is food, but we're—I'm out of meat. Alfred Jones used to do all the hunting when my aunt was alive. He offered to continue, but his terms of barter were—" Rachel clamped her mouth shut. When they both looked expectantly at her, she finished weakly, "They were not acceptable."

She set the tray down on a low table and lifted Douglas's scotch and water. Ice tinkled in his glass, sounding abnormally loud. "Here, my chief."

Douglas flashed a wicked smile, and she wondered if he knew how dangerously attractive he looked when he did that. She swallowed nervously. He took his time reaching for the drink, letting his finger slide along hers.

Rachel picked up a cold beer still in the bottle. Quietly, she said, "William," as she handed the bottle to William. He smiled and she couldn't meet his gaze for long. His fingers also bumped hers.

Rachel's nerves tingled and she absently rubbed her fingers where the men had touched her. She became painfully aware of the silence filling the room and the isolation beyond the cabin. Slowly, she sat, grabbing her own drink—beer in a mug with a slice of lime.

"Mr. Jones wanted to trade services, did he?" Douglas asked in his softly accented voice. The predatory smile still curved his lips, and his dark eyes bore into hers. "I don't blame him for trying."

"Oh, ah." Rachel quickly drank her beer. When she'd downed half the glass, she said, "I'm sorry there isn't much to do, but you're welcome to run the forest. This is protected land. We do get the rare trespasser now and again, but usually it's a lost hiker or college kids out looking for adventure." She was sorry she mentioned it. The idea of them shifting, all powerful, and by all rights naked, caused her insides to quiver. Damn it! She'd just had sex and suddenly she was feeling like she needed to do it again.

She looked at William. He was the natural choice. They'd slept together once already and he wasn't her chief. Plus, William was the first shifter she had ever been with. His expression was guarded. What was he thinking about?

Still… She glanced at Douglas. His shaded expression and parted lips held massive appeal.

"Trying to get rid of us, lass?" Douglas asked, grinning.

"N-no," she denied. "If you don't want to roam the forest, there's a library through there," she pointed towards the side of the fireplace, "or if you're tired, rooms are upstairs. They might be a bit dusty from little use, but the linen is clean. I wasn't expecting visitors."

Side by side, the men's differences became apparent. William's chest rose and fell as if the beast pressed against the inside of his flesh, ready to rip out. His eyes were narrowed, and he stared at her as if he could smell the longing unfurling in her sex. There was a great restraint in him, a forced calmness that had to come from years of practice. It was something she recognized because she had to do the same thing. The wolf was hard to control even in human form.

Douglas, with his soft, Gaelic brogue and

perfectly tailored appearance, moved like a king used to sitting before his noble court. Every gesture was deliberate and refined. He sipped his drink, as if savoring the taste of the liquor on his gorgeous lips. Despite this, Rachel detected more than a hint of the wild in him. The fact he had a bad boy reputation didn't help matters. He may look calm, but her chief knew all about letting the wild out.

"What about a phone?" William asked.

"There is a land line, but your cellular phones should work here. Aunt Elvie, um, made a deal to have a private tower set up on the mountain," she said.

Both men smiled. William said, "I think I would have liked this Elvie. Was that her field I smelled in the forest?"

"The pot? Oh yeah. That was Elvie. I don't smoke myself."

"Dulls the senses," Douglas said.

"How did you come to live with your aunt?" William sat forward intently.

She felt like she was under interrogation. "Don't the clans keep records of that information? Are you a census taker?"

"Hardly," William muttered.

"We're just talking," Douglas said. "And the clan records are not complete, especially for the

Americas. Shifters by nature are wild and not prone to reporting births and deaths as they're encouraged to do. The last accounting was nearly two hundred years ago."

"Two hundred and fifty for the Cononious," William said. "Perhaps it is time to rectify that."

"Agreed." Douglas nodded. They both turned to Rachel expectantly. Apparently, they thought to start the new accounting of the clans with her family history.

"My parents were killed in a car accident. Elvie was the only family who could take me in." Before they could pry further and continue their inquisition, she asked, "And what brings you two to America?"

"We are here on official business," William said.

"We?" She glanced at the chief and then back to the man who spoke. "You work for the chief?"

Douglas laughed. The expression of merriment flooded his face and filled his dark eyes. When he tried to answer, he only laughed harder.

William had the opposite reaction. He frowned, looking at his palms. Douglas reached for the other man's hand, lifting it up so she could see William's scarred palm. Rachel stiffened, whispering, "The Cononious chief." Then she looked at Douglas. "And the Duncanis chief." Swallowing nervously, she realized just how powerful these two men were. Combined, they ruled every shifter on the planet. "Am I in trouble? Is this because I didn't keep the sanctuary open full time? I swear I didn't realize I was breaking any laws." Then pointing at them both, she said, "And that snake shifter was way out of line. He came here right after my aunt's funeral trying to lay lover rights to me, and when I refused, he threatened to take this land from me. I was only defending myself when I cut him. I swear, I could have done much worse, and he deserved much worse, but I refrained."

Both men grinned.

"You are not in trouble," Douglas said. "We're only here for a place to stay that is away from the cities. Even chiefs need time away from the clans."

William shared a secret look with Douglas. "No one will think to look for us here."

"Not unless we tell them to," Douglas answered the man.

"Oh. Well, how long do you think you'll be here? You can have the lodge for as long as you need. I can stay in the city." She stood. "In fact, I'll go now. If I jog, I'll make it back tonight and will have supplies delivered to you in the morning."

"I'll go for supplies," William said.

"Yes." Douglas nodded in agreement. "We

wish for you to stay here with us. We are not accustomed to taking over people's homes without them in it."

"And we can fill in your education where your Aunt Elvie left off. The mountain sanctuaries in America are few and we need to ensure this one is maintained properly." William finished his beer before setting the bottle down. He held his hand out to Douglas. "Your keys. I didn't bring a car."

Douglas reached into his pocket and handed them over. William nodded at them, looking for a long time at Rachel before moving to leave. When he was gone, she asked, "Is he all right? I mean, I know I don't know him, but he seemed upset."

"He'll be fine, lass," Douglas dismissed. "Nothing for you to worry over."

"Well, I suppose I should see to your rooms. I'm sure they're not anything like you're used to. I'll try to tidy up, though." She made a move to go to the stairs, thinking to run away from him. In the distance, she heard a motor start. It was a low hum, almost impossible to hear over the soft background noise of the generator.

Douglas moved right behind her, following her up. She glanced around the hall, trying to figure out where to put them. It didn't seem right to stick them in her aunt's old room. Then, going to the biggest guest room, she opened the door. A large, king-size bed dominated the space. It matched the dark wood of an antique dresser and oversized chest. A light layer of dust coated the wood.

"Will this work?" she asked.

"Perfectly." He stood a little too close.

"If you would like to wait downstairs while I dust—"

"No need, I assure you," he interrupted.

She felt the heat radiating from his body, as if calling her to lean into him. Rachel studied the floor. She'd just had sex with one stranger. She wouldn't be repeating the performance. She backed slowly away, moving out the opened door. "I'll leave you to get settled then. Towels are in the bathroom down the hall on the left if you'd like a shower. The generator's been on for a while so the water should be warm."

He watched her with his dark, probing eyes. When he looked at her like that, he seemed to fill up the entire room. "Care to join me?"

She shook her head once in denial and hurried from his sight.

❧

DOUGLAS GRINNED. EVERY PART OF HIM WANTED to go after her and play the role of predator to her prey. He resisted. Charging after a woman like a beast wasn't his style—at least not at first.

He whistled lightly, stripping out of his clothes before walking towards the shower. Rachel was on her way up the stairs, carrying blankets. His grin widened as he stopped whistling. She skidded to a stop and stared at his naked body. When she didn't look away, his cock twitched with interest. She gasped and quickly spun around. Douglas chuckled and continued on towards the bathroom.

EIGHT

RACHEL PEERED OUT THE WINDOW, USING ALL
her senses to detect William's presence. He'd been
gone for hours, more hours than a trip to town
should have taken. Though, seeing him shifted
and knowing he was a chief, she wasn't worried
about anything happening to him. She was more
worried about being left alone with Douglas. The
man was altogether too sexy for his own good. As
she had listened to the shower, she couldn't help
but imagine beads of water flowing down that
tight flesh, caressing each curve, molding wet
rivulets and trailing down hot crevices.

If she was going to take a shifter lover, and she
wasn't convinced she would, she would have to
pick the man she'd already slept with. Wouldn't
she? It's not like she could have two. Rachel

glanced over her shoulder to where Douglas lounged on the couch, book in one hand, drink in the other. He pretended not to look at her, but she felt his attention.

"No one is out there," Douglas said, not looking up. "I promise to tell you if anyone comes within a ten-mile radius. You might as well take a seat."

Rachel inched slowly across the room. "I think I need to buy a television for this place and some DVDs. Aunt Elvie had dial-up internet put in through the phone line, but it's impossible to surf the net with dial-up these days and I canceled the service."

"Hmm," Douglas answered. He flipped a page in his book.

Rachel sighed, eyeing the room. Things had been so much different when Elvie was there. Rachel had never noticed the silence of the woods because there were always people around—telling stories, building metal sculptures in the yard, painting, writing, shifting, drinking and partying. She missed the noise, the smell of beer and cooking food. On evenings like this, someone would have the smoker going outside and the mesquite scent would hang thick in the air. A wave of sadness washed over her.

Instantly, Douglas's book was down by his side and he stood. "What is it?"

"What is what?" She tilted her head to the side and listened to the distance.

"I felt your sadness. What is it?" He didn't move.

"Oh, it's nothing. I was thinking of the silence." She studied her hands. "This house always had so much life. It drained out the day Elvie died. People tried to stay, but she was the force behind this isolated world. Without her, it was too depressing, and one by one everyone wandered away like the wild animals they are. I think that's why I don't live out here. The silence is too much. I can't stand it beyond a couple days at a time."

"Silence or loneliness?" He moved to sit beside her.

"Sometimes I think they're one and the same," she admitted.

"You don't have to be lonely. You could be the new life in this place. It would be what you make of it," he said. "Shifters would come if you opened the doors and welcomed them."

She looked at him, suddenly realizing how close he sat to her. "Elvie had a kind of magic I don't possess. She was a light that drew people in like a beacon in the night."

His hand brushed her thigh, and she felt the tingle of it all the way up her body. She looked at that hand, watching it draw a slow circle up her leg, imagining she could feel the scar on his palm through her clothing. For a long moment, he didn't answer as his hand made its way seductively higher. She could smell the unmistakable interest of his desire. It washed over her, the pheromone nearly undetectable but incredibly potent. His hand slid over her lap to her hip. Fingers worked over her side, pulling her gradually closer to him.

His breath fanned over her cheek and ear. She forced her eyes away from where he'd touched her leg, away from the tingling nerves that remained there. She looked at his waist, not surprised to find the thick arousal pressing from beneath his slacks. She'd seen the thickness of his cock, the tight flesh of his body.

No one would know. She was an adult. He was… She swallowed nervously. He was a chief.

Perhaps it was the power of his position or the forbidden temptation of it that fueled her lust. Or, more likely still, it was his cologne-scented, pheromone-infused smell and fiery heat. Either way, she found her hand moving onto his hard thigh. Caressing him as he had her, she didn't stop on her journey up. Rachel kept her eyes down, watching her fingers glide closer to the hidden prize.

His breathing became labored as she cupped his erection through the clothes. She explored the thick length of it. Her pussy ached, so wet and ready, as if remembering the intense orgasm William had given her and wanting the sensations again by any means necessary.

How could she do this? She rubbed his cock harder. How could she not?

She didn't belong to any man. She could be with whomever she wanted. Douglas pushed his hand up into her shirt. Rachel unfastened his pants only to discover silk boxers. The elegant, black material suited him. He tugged at her cotton pants, easily removing them from her hips along with her panties when she lifted up from the seat. Her naked ass pressed into the leather couch. Douglas slipped a hand over her sex and rubbed.

Rachel pulled his boxers off his erection so she could return the favor. She stroked him, growing more excited with each pass. His finger pressed into her wet slit before dipping up into her body. She breathed hard, kicking the pants off completely and spreading her legs. Pleasure built where he touched, as if he knew exactly how to make a woman come. She bet he did. A man who looked like him probably had tons of experience.

His hand pulled away and she moaned in

protest. He lifted up, pulled his boxers off his hips and then pushed her leg to the side so she was forced to turn on the couch. As she fell on her back, he came over her.

A low growl sounded in the back of his throat, and she saw the silver power flecking his eyes. He drew himself to her, as if propelled forward by urgent need. His cock rubbed up against her sex, not dipping inside, but simply gliding along her pussy. He groaned.

"Ah, your heat," he whispered, as if that statement said more than it did. He jerked her shirt up and her bra cups down to bare her breasts. His lips parted, but he didn't speak. Instead, he reached between them and angled his cock for penetration.

At first, he moved slowly, filling her so she could detect every hot inch. His thrusts were more fluid that William's had been. William had been wild and hard. Douglas was smooth and controlled. He lifted above her, pressing his hips fully to her as he gave her his entire length.

"Oh, heaven," he murmured. "Pure, wet heaven."

She pulled his shirt out of the way so she could explore his waist and hips. Rachel pressed up as she pulled his hips down. He slid deeper, almost painfully so. Where William's cock had been thicker, Douglas's was longer—though she'd definitely consider both well endowed.

Stop comparing them, her brain scolded, but she couldn't help it. The differences were too marked.

His hips rolled in small circles as he thrust. His arousal hit all the right spots. Muscles flexed as he put his whole delectable body into it. Her bra pressed her breasts up. The nipples ached for attention.

"Oh," she sighed, "you feel really good. Don't stop. Just like that."

He obeyed, repeating a particularly elegant move of his hips.

She sighed harder. "Where did you learn to do this? Oh. My. Oh, fuck. There!"

He grinned, a truly dominant and wicked look, as if he knew how good he was. "You like that, do you?" He did it harder and she gasped. "How about that? You like that?" She managed a weak sound of agreement. Suddenly, he pulled himself out to her entrance and stopped.

Her eyes widened in surprise and she tried to force him to continue. "Not yet."

"You want my cock?"

She nodded. "Mm."

"Say it. Say you want my cock. Say you need it."

"I want it. I need it," she whispered. Rachel pulled hard, trying to get him back inside her.

"Yell it," he demanded. "I want to hear you scream for it."

She opened her mouth but nothing readily came out. Her pussy ached. She'd been so close. She needed him to continue. When she didn't answer, he began to move, as if pushing way from her.

"I need your cock," she cried. "Fuck me, my chief!"

He grinned, but she had little time to wonder at the victory in his eyes as he plunged forward. Her nerves stung and he quickened his previous pace. Oh, but it was good.

"Yes," she yelled, not caring at this point. All she knew was that she would die if he stopped. "There!"

His body tightened and he bit his lip. "Come for me, lass. That's it."

She came, shaking violently beneath him. He kept going, riding out the sensation several more times before letting loose. His yell was one of release and victory. For a long moment, he stayed inside her.

"There's a good lass," he whispered, finally pulling out.

She wasn't sure she appreciated his words, but

was too far gone in the aftermath of pleasure to argue. Closing her eyes, she didn't dare move.

❖

DOUGLAS BREATHED HARD, LETTING THE pleasure of release claim him. Rachel lay sprawled on the couch, thoroughly spent. Grinning wickedly, he was far from finished with her. Since he sat up, he could see over the back of the couch. He looked towards the window a few feet away. William stood on the other side of the glass, eyes narrowed and chest heaving. Douglas had heard him coming and had made her scream on purpose. He wanted the man to be jealous, just as he had been. Douglas wanted William to know that he fucked Rachel and that she came for him, just as she'd come for William earlier.

Oh, but she'd been sweet. He didn't want to share her. The only drawback to letting William hear her pleasure was that he knew Douglas had taken his turn. Now Douglas would be forced by honor to stand down until William found his pleasure. It was the agreement they had made after all, and one they would continue to honor until Rachel dictated otherwise. It was her pleasure they sought, and it was her command they would follow.

He glanced down, not wanting to wait. Already his shaft was starting to lift. Rachel's eyes were on him. She looked down her body to his arousal and licked her lips. He swallowed hard, seeing her intent. Silver filled her eyes and he detected the creature he carried to be close to the surface. She wanted to suck him. Gods help him, he wanted to let her.

Douglas glanced at the window, almost ready to plead with William to let him have more. William, as if sensing what was about to happen was suddenly pushing through the door. Rachel gasped in shock. She quickly pulled down her shirt, stretching it so it hid her thighs as she looked for her pants.

"Wi-William," she stammered. "This... It's not what you—I mean, it wouldn't matter—that is...was...is...rather not..." She moaned weakly. Her cheeks flamed with red.

"Don't let me stop you," William muttered, his tone a little dark.

Rachel must have missed the slight bit of sarcasm in his tone because she automatically looked back to Douglas's cock, as if she was being instructed to suck him while William watched.

"Oh no, I mean, I can't..." She held her pants to her chest, not bending over to put them on. She backed away so she could look at both of them.

"I'm not normally so, um, sexual. I mean, in Europe you might all be into watching and, um, well, I'm not normally so…"

"Sexual?" William supplied.

"I would disagree," Douglas said. They both eyed her retreat. He felt a matching beast within William. They both wanted to go after her.

William reached for his shirt and pulled it over his head. "We can smell your desire, Rachel. Don't think we can't. Don't leave. Stay. Let me pleasure you however you wish." He unfastened his jeans. "Or if it's a cock you want to suck…" His words trailed off as he pushed his jeans down. Douglas watched, unable to move. His arousal throbbed jealously, wanting to be the one to feel her soft lips first.

"That wouldn't be, ah…" Still, she wasn't running away from them.

William fisted his cock. "Do mine and then his if you must."

She licked her lips, glancing back and forth. Douglas couldn't help himself. He touched his cock and stroked lazily. He wanted to speak but didn't interrupt William. If the man was willing to let him stay in the room during his turn, Douglas would not complain.

"Ah." Rachel looked back and forth between them. Then, turning, she sprinted up the stairs.

"Well done. Way to scare her off," Douglas said sarcastically, letting go of his hard shaft. With Rachel gone, he'd lost interest in continuing. "You are such a dog."

"You're just jealous that I'm bold enough to offer, cat," William answered. He strode toward the door. "The generator sounds funny. I'm going to go check on it."

That's when Douglas realized William only did what he'd done out of anger. He hadn't appreciated being forced to hear Rachel's cries of pleasure with another man. Muttering to himself, Douglas said, "Stupid mutt. You'll chase her away from us both with your rash actions."

NINE

Rachel stood naked before her second story bedroom window. After the little performance in the living room, she needed to get away from the two shifters. She'd seen the look in their eyes. They were having a supernatural pissing contest over her. Both of them wanted her to choose between them. It wasn't going to happen. Douglas was her clan's chief. Surely he would have some expectations of her. William was raw and powerful. She knew he was no one she should mess with. The last thing she wanted to do was be the bait between two very hungry animals.

"They can stroke each other for all I care," she muttered, torn between anger and extreme embarrassment. She tried to tell herself that it wasn't her fault, that the men were carrying some powerful pheromones she couldn't resist. In truth, that idea was an excuse. She'd been weak. She'd wanted them both. She'd given in to her very pent-up desires. They had exploded out of her, and she only had herself to blame for her actions. It wasn't the sex that embarrassed her so much as the idea she'd taken two shifter chief lovers so recent to each other.

Rachel threw her clothes out the window and watched them land on the sharp decorative stones below. Then, perching on the window ledge, she spread her arms wide. She listened, making sure the men weren't coming up the stairs. Then, keeping her arms extended, she dove towards the earth. Her flesh tingled, and she felt the air hitting her arms and legs seconds before her body took flight. The shift was painful, but fast, as she swooped past the ground. Her talons grasped her clothes into tight fists, and she flapped her long wings. Her heart raced and she knew that she couldn't hold the shift for long. Already her body felt as if it was going to explode from within her bird form. Elvie had been the one to teach her how to fly, but said Rachel did not take to it naturally because she had too much energy pent up inside the smaller body. It was not easy carrying multiple forms inside one person.

Rachel shivered and swooped closer to the

trail, dropping the clothes in an effort to land. Because the shift was so hard, she had never perfected the landing. Talons burst into feet and she was thrown forward. All she could do was tuck her head and somersault until she came to a stop.

Groaning and a little bruised, she rolled onto her stomach and pushed to her feet. She limped towards her clothes and somehow managed to pull them on with shaking hands. The instant she was dressed, her sneakers hit the ground and she was off and running—well, limp running anyway. She might never turn back. Let the naked chiefs take over her home. After the way they acted, she never wanted to see them again. Hell, after the way *she* acted, she never wanted to face them again.

The night air felt great against her arms and legs, and soon she was sprinting. Her cramped muscles stretched, the bruises faded and the scrapes healed. Her heart thumped in time with her steps. Everything came into perfect alignment as the miles melted beneath her feet. Her head cleared the further she ran. Maybe she had been too quick to blame herself for being weak. She realized her home must have been filled with male pheromones as they competed for her attention. Now that she could think clearly, it really was the only explanation for her mindless behavior.

"Damn shifter men," she grumbled breath-lessly. Without Elvie's weekly cleansing spells, no wonder she'd been overwhelmed.

A strange smell penetrated her nose and she skidded to a halt. Smoke. Dust. Fire. It came from behind her. Her eyes blazing with the beast, she turned and ran back the way she'd come, harder and faster. The subtle glow of orange outlined the tops of the trees. The fire was big.

They torched the house. She ran from them, and the two royal pains-in-the-ass chiefs torched her house out of spite?

She growled, leaping as her body shifted into the form of a wolf. On all fours, she'd be able to dart through the forest in half the time. The orange light turned to heat. Smoke tickled her nose long before she could see it billowing over the earth from the flame box of the lodge home. She stopped short of a tree line, restlessly pawing the earth.

"Rachel!" Douglas yelled, running around the home as he looked to the second story. William stumbled out of the front door, holding his arm over his face. When he appeared, Douglas ran into the fiery home.

"Rachel! Can you make it to the window? We can catch you!" William coughed. His voice was hoarse. They were looking for her. But why, if they were the ones who set the fire? Unless…

They weren't alone in the forest. Rachel lowered her head and scanned the trees. Yellow firelight glinted off a pair of eyes across the yard. She growled, charging. William saw her and yelled, "Douglas!"

Douglas burst from the house. "Did you find her?"

"There!" William cried.

From the corner of her eye, she saw both of them sniff the air. In unison, they yelled, "Rachel!" The men ran after her. She ignored them, concentrating on the intruder. Primal thoughts of tearing flesh and marking territory filled her. She neared the creature, a mountain lion, and leapt. The cat was more agile than she'd anticipated, and claws slashed viciously at her face, slicing the flesh. She caught a paw briefly between her teeth and tasted blood. Then the cat was gone, disappearing into the trees.

Rachel tried to move, but blood dripped over her eye and she couldn't see. She whined, lying on the ground so she could cover her face with her paw. William sniffed at her, nudging her with his shifted nose. Douglas leapt into the woods in the form of a black panther, trying to chase down the mountain lion.

Rachel pushed to her feet, feeling dizzy. The heat from the burning house drew her attention. She looked in time to see the second story collapse into the first. Suddenly, the generator shed exploded, a loud boom that made her jolt.

She swayed, falling to the ground once more. Rachel closed her eyes, letting darkness take her. She didn't want to see any more.

TEN

William glanced into the rearview mirror, watching Douglas as he cradled an unconscious Rachel in his arms. He sped through the forest, listening to his cellular phone ring.

"Hello?"

"Magda, it's me. We're switching locations. We were at that forest sanctuary near where my flight landed. It's on the old maps. Someone set the lodge on fire while we were inside. We need—"

"I'll handle the fire," she assured him, her voice calm. He heard the clicking of computer keys as she spoke. William didn't even bother asking how she would take care of it from the other side of the ocean. She just would. "I'll send you coordinates to a safe house and let our friends know you're on the way."

"I have two with me," he said, meeting William's eyes.

"Two?" she asked. He wasn't sure if she sounded disappointed or simply preoccupied.

William said, "It was the sanctuary woman's home that burned and my," he glanced at Douglas, "counterpart."

"Very well. For the sake of appearances, I'll order the lodge rebuilt. Make sure she knows that we expect no grievances from her on the matter. For all we know, it was because of her that the accident happened in the first place."

"You assume a lot from an ocean away," he grumbled.

"I will text you the safe house location." Magda didn't deign to answer his comment. "Who set the fire, boy?"

"Mountain lion. Female," he answered. "I didn't recognize who it was and she got away."

"Ah yes, that must be St. Joan. She's an American claw for hire with connections to a couple families here in the UK. Has a flare for setting things on fire. I'll check into it." More computer keys clicked in the background.

"An assassination attempt?"

"What?" Douglas said from the back seat.

"Claw for hire. UK family connections," William told him quickly before turning back to his conversation.

"I warned you when you left that you would have to be careful with your location. Until you are married, properly, and in possession of an heir, you are in a dangerous position. There are those who would be glad to challenge you for your throne. And if they can see to it that you have an accident before that time…" She sighed heavily. "I'll have bodyguards on the next flight."

"What's happening?"

"Do we want bodyguards?" William asked.

"No," Douglas said.

"No guards, Magda," William said into the phone.

"But—" she began to protest.

"Tell whoever you're talking to that we're coming home," Douglas said. "I'll have my people arrange the private jet. It's stashed nearby."

"Magda, get a place ready. We're coming home."

"All three of you?" she asked.

"Yes, all three of us." William met Douglas's gaze. The man nodded once and a silent understanding passed between them. "Travel arrangements are taken care of."

❖

RACHEL'S MIND DRIFTED THROUGH A FOG. SHE vaguely registered being carried, being in a car, being in pain and then not in pain until finally she was oddly numb. It was almost like she'd been dosed with painkillers. By the time she could open her eyes long enough to concentrate, she had no idea where she was. The room was small, with rounded, white walls and a narrow bed. Small windows lined the walls on each side. She frowned. If she wasn't mistaken, it looked like the inside of an airplane.

She reached for her face. The flesh was healed. Crawling out of the bed, she limped to a window and pushed up the shade. Clouds stretched before her. The plane was airborne.

The stiffness of her muscles made her steps a little zombie-like as she crossed to the door. Someone had dressed her in what equated to blue doctor scrubs. She heard William and Douglas whispering as she pressed on the latch. The sound instantly stopped when she entered the lounge area. They each sat in thick, camel-colored chairs with drinks in hand. The room looked like the pimped-out private jet of a rock star—flat screen TV, stocked bar, leather chairs. All that was missing was a bunch of drunk, scantily clad chicks running around, and a smarmy manager trying to get some action off a drunken groupie.

"What have you done?" she demanded. Their answering expressions were a cross between relief and guilt.

"You should not be up," William said. He wore blue jeans and a white button-down shirt. She could see the outline of his undershirt beneath it.

"The cuts were deep. You need rest." Douglas stood, offering his chair though there were others in the cabin. His dark slacks and a gray designer shirt were in stark contrast to the other man's relaxed style.

One elegant and one primal. They were different, yet both powerful, both beautiful, both sexy as sin. Her body tingled. She wanted both of them, and by the look in their eyes, they wanted her. Why was she resisting? The shifter world did not judge as the human world did. The human world did not have the passion the shifter world did.

Rachel glanced towards a small window, seeing the clouds. "What happened? Where are we going?"

"Someplace safe," Douglas assured her.

"The lodge was lost. People were sent to tend the fire, but there was nothing left." William's manner a little more blunt than the other man's. "We have men looking into it, but we're pretty sure the attempt was on our lives, not yours. I've already dispatched builders to the area. They will clean up and rebuild the sanctuary."

"So you thought it best to bring me with you while I'm waiting on the repairs?" Rachel questioned. Douglas and William both nodded. "You thought it best to bring me with *you*, the *targets* of an assassination attempt?"

Smart thinking, fellas.

Their expressions fell.

"Nothing will happen to you," Douglas said.

"Nothing," William asserted.

Everything, Rachel thought, as she looked at them.

"We know that rebuilding the cabin won't be the same as your childhood home," Douglas said.

"If there is anything we can do to make up that loss to you, simply name it," William added.

"Name it and it's yours," Douglas agreed. "Anything."

She didn't want to think about the fire or her childhood memories that were lost to it. Not right now. Her muscles ached and her head was a little dizzy. "I can't think about this right now. I need a beer."

William was on his feet, instantly going to the

stocked bar to fulfill her request. He seemed eager to do it.

"Is there anything to eat?" she asked. "I would have healed faster if you'd just let me eat and run."

Douglas crossed to a small cabinet.

"Speaking of shifting," William began.

"Trout?" Douglas finished the thought with an arch of his brow. "Diluted blood?"

Rachel didn't speak for a long moment. She hadn't meant for them to see her in shifted form. Her secret was out. Both men looked expectantly at her, one holding a beer, the other holding a big sandwich wrapped in cellophane. To her great surprise, she realized she wasn't upset about them knowing. They were the shifter chiefs and they looked ready to do her every bidding. She felt protected and strangely powerful.

"Why would I tell you what I am? You were a stranger following me in a bookstore," she answered.

"I would follow you anywhere, lass," Douglas stated smoothly.

She felt a small thrill at his words. Being alone with them in the cabin had been tough. Alone in a plane? She couldn't very well jump out of a window. Feeling hot, she glanced at the window. Could she make it? If she fell in human form until she was a few feet from the ground, then shifted, then possibly…

"I would do whatever you commanded," William said, holding out the beer.

With shaking hands, she took it. His finger reached out to caress hers. Feeling a little light-headed, she asked, "Whatever I commanded?"

William nodded.

"I would as well," Douglas said, unwrapping the sandwich to give it to her.

Rachel took it. Her skin began to tingle. She moved back towards the small room. Right before she turned to enter the onboard bedroom, she stated, "I am a little sore."

She heard shuffling behind her and tried not to laugh. One man pushed the other aside and she heard a loud thump. Rachel crawled onto the bed, lying on her stomach. She took a quick drink and set the beer bottle on the floor. Then, propping up on her elbows, she took a bite of the sandwich. The bed shifted by her left leg and then her right. She took another bite. "Mm, so good. I feel like I haven't been fed in days."

"We fed you," Douglas assured her. "Broth."

A hand touched her right ankle, massaging up her leg beneath the loose pants. Seconds later, another hand touched her left ankle, sliding upward to the back of her knee. The rougher texture of their palms made her think of their royal brands. Her blood stirred, pumping fiercely through her veins. Their hands moved in agonizingly slow caresses, mimicking each other as they slid up and down her leg.

Rachel tried to keep eating, but her breathing became too ragged. She dropped the sandwich on the floor next to the beer. She heard a thud and the sound of liquor sloshing out of the bottle, but didn't care. Hands fisted the material behind her knees and pulled. They bared her ass easily, forcing the unresisting material down off her hips.

Her eyes stared forward, but her attention was focused behind her. Soft breath fanned her flesh, tickling the back of her calf. Warm lips followed, near her ankle first, trailing up her leg to the sensitive flesh at the back of her knee. Hands massaged into the other leg, pressing deeply. Her chest heaved with ragged breaths. Her heart beat faster. She twisted her fingers into the bedding, which was still messed up from her earlier rest.

She squirmed on the bed, lifting her hips slightly as a mouth kissed the bottom curve of her ass. The way teeth grazed flesh, she knew the mouth to be William's. He bit lightly. The hands left her and the unmistakable whisper of clothing followed. Soon, cooler lips replaced the warm, only they too heated quickly against her flesh.

Douglas's kisses were smooth, and he traced gentle lines with his tongue. She heard William undress before joining them on the bed once more.

Rachel still didn't turn to look. The sight of two gorgeous, naked men might be her undoing. She became mindless under the euphoria of their caresses. Hands and lips moved over her ass, down her legs, up her back. They pulled at her loose shirt until she tugged it over her head and threw it aside. Her naked breasts rubbed into the bed. One massaged her back, the other her legs. Moisture gathered between her thighs, pooling along her sex.

Douglas stretched out next to her on the bed. She glanced at him from the corner of her eye. He lifted her hair, pushing it aside so he could kiss her neck. Shivers racked her from where his lips touched, so light and warm. Lips trailed to his jaw, and she found herself turning towards him. He grinned before drawing her mouth to his. His tongue traced the seam of her mouth, urging her lips to part. The thick, naked length of his cock brushed against her stomach and he moaned.

Behind her, William's hands moved up her thighs. She parted them automatically, allowing him access. Fingers grazed along her sex. She moaned softly into Douglas's mouth. William stroked her clit as his body sandwiched her against Douglas's. The pleasure overwhelmed her senses until she could no longer tell whose hands were where. They were on her breasts, her pussy, her back, and ass. She reached behind her, taking William by the hip and pulling him closer. Her legs tangled with his.

"Mm." Douglas pulled his mouth away. "Turn around."

Their hands turned her and she faced William. His kiss was harder, rougher. He pulled her leg over his hip and his cock brushed against her sex. She hesitated, unsure how this should work—with two men and only one of her. Douglas, as if answering her unasked questions, moved his hand down the back of her thigh, as if encouraging her to take William first.

William grabbed her breast, pinching the nipple. She arched back into him and reached for his cock as William brought himself along her entrance. He kissed her hard as he thrust inside her. The position didn't allow for him to go deep.

She was forced to let go of Douglas's arousal as he moved to press his cock along the cleft of her ass. He pressed into her, controlling her thrusts onto William's cock with the pressure of his hips. William moved his hard kisses along her neck, biting lightly. She wanted more, wanted him deeper and harder. The slow pace was agonizing torture.

With a groan, she pushed her body up from between them so she could straddle William. He made a loud noise of approval, his silver tinted eyes penetrating her with their hot desire.

Douglas, now abandoned from her heat, stretched out on his side next to them breathing hard. Seeing his long, lean body, so sleek with sweat and muscles, ready to be taken, she reached for him. She raked her nails down his chest and he moved to lie on his back. He didn't touch William, but lay close to him.

Rachel fisted his cock, hoping to give him a little pleasure. She stroked Douglas as William fucked her, hard and wild, his hips bucking her up and down. Tension built and she threw her head back. Douglas's hand covered hers, keeping her stroking him when her rhythm faltered.

William grabbed her hips. His words came in short bursts, "Ah, fuck, fuck, fuck…"

Rachel's body jerked as she came. It felt so good she nearly cried with the pleasure. Douglas continued to move her hand, and she felt a tremor wash over him. She watched their faces, seeing their pleasure, their desire. Suddenly, Douglas released her. He hadn't finished and she felt bad for it. William found release, coming inside her.

She was so wet, almost sticky now that he'd found his climax.

Breathing hard, she felt weak and powerful at the same time. Douglas had pushed up on his elbows, as if to get up, but seeing his hard erection, she moved to straddle him. Her pussy was already wet. She'd come hard, but the idea of making Douglas join their climax excited her. She instantly reached for him, taking him in her slick hot pussy. He slid easily and she rode him, giving as much effort as she'd given the man before him.

William watched, licking his lips as he eyed her breasts. He knelt beside her, leaning forward to suck a peaked nipple. A shockwave passed from her chest down to her pussy and back up again.

"That's it, lass," Douglas urged. "Let me have you."

She tried to hold off, waiting for him to come, but his accented words were too much. She came, shaking violently. Seconds later, he let loose, coming inside her. She was too far gone to care where they spilled their seed. Shifters did not impregnate easily, and they didn't have the same sexual concerns as humans.

She fell forward against his chest. His heart beat hard against her. William fell to the bed, lazily smiling as if he'd managed to recuperate as she took Douglas. He reached for his cock, stroking the flaccid length, encouraging its interest. When she looked down his body and saw what he was doing, she moaned weakly. "My turn again," he said, his words gruff. "We're not done with you."

Douglas stroked her back gently. He was still embedded inside her.

"Come," William urged. "Give me that mouth. I want to feel your lips." His eyes flashed, drawing her forward like a magnet. He was inviting the animal in her out to play and the animal accepted. She licked her lips and pushed off Douglas's body. She surged forward, every thought gone but the primal, violent urges inside her.

She took his cock in her mouth, sucking it deep. There was something animalistic to the way his body moved and tensed—potent, raw, male. He groaned, pressing his hand into her head. Moaning, she adjusted onto her hands and knees. Douglas came up behind her, and she felt his mouth on her ass cheek. William hardened to full capacity in her mouth. She sucked harder. He tasted good, salty and sweet.

Douglas drew his body up, taking full advantage of her position. He shoved his cock into her hard, not testing the depths as he controlled her hips. He seemed to grow inside her. Her nails dug into William's thighs. He jerked, finding release.

Rachel gasped for breath. Douglas pumped into her from behind, and they soon met with trembling climax. She collapsed on William's chest, hearing his heart pound beneath her cheek. Douglas stretched behind her, touching her hip. She reached for his hand, holding it lightly as she closed her eyes. William's even breaths lulled her to sleep.

ELEVEN

As worldly as she wished to appear, Rachel found herself feeling quite the opposite. She blushed in embarrassment as she tried to untangle her limbs from a sleeping Douglas. William was gone, but the imprint of his body was still visible on the covers. And even as she told herself she wouldn't spend all day thinking, *what have I done?*, that was exactly the thought that ran through her brain.

Her inner ears popped, and she looked towards the small window. The plane was descending. Douglas moaned and sleepily reached for her. He tried to pull her back down.

"We're landing," Rachel said, evading his hold. When she swung her legs over the side, her foot landed in a wet puddle. The beer bottle and sandwich were gone, but the floor was still wet from the spill. She reached for her clothes and began to tug them on. "Where exactly are we landing?"

"UK," Douglas answered with a yawn. She stumbled a little, trying to keep balance as the plane angled. "Someplace safe until…" He didn't finish as he reached for his clothes.

"Until?" she prompted. She'd never been to Europe, and this wasn't exactly the way she envisioned taking such a trip. Considering much of what she owned was now burnt to the ground, including her passport, credit cards and driver's license, she wasn't sure how exactly they planned on sneaking her through UK customs. And how exactly was she going to get back into the US when the time came for her to go home?

"Damn," he cursed, bracing himself. "They should have told us to prepare for landing."

Rachel leaned against the wall, holding on to a ledge. She closed her eyes tight, hating the turbulent feeling of descent as it jarred her body. She much preferred to be in control. Thinking of Douglas and William, she knew she had never been more out of control in her life.

❧

WILLIAM STEPPED OFF THE PLANE. THE PRIVATE runway was surrounded by English countryside, thick trees and dense shrubs that gave way to an open meadow. The tall grasses were green and spotted with random flowers. He'd missed the smell of home, the fresh air and nature. America hadn't been bad, but it smelled differently. This was home. It was part of him. He glanced at the plane. And he was going to share it with Rachel.

He jogged across the landing strip towards Magda. She stood, holding a briefcase. Her stern face gave nothing away, well, nothing to an outsider. William could see her concern. She looked past him, as if waiting to get a glimpse of the American woman under his protection.

While Rachel slept, he'd had a long talk with Douglas. They would share her, so long as she would have them, and if she would have them, they would offer her everything. Neither of them could imagine a more perfect match to two chiefs. A surge of protectiveness washed over him. With her strong blood, the people would accept her, or would come to in time.

"Well?" Magda asked, handing him the briefcase.

"We're safe. Chief Douglas is in the plane with Rachel." He glanced down to the case, unable to shake the feeling of being a kid about to be scolded. Magda was the only person who had that effect on him.

"Rachel?" She gave him a pointed look, knowing full well the influence she had on the younger shifter.

"Do not pretend you haven't already looked up everything there is to know about her." William lifted the case. "I assume the fruits of your research are in here?"

"It is," Magda nodded. "She is American. Her family—"

"I don't care about that," William said. "I know what I need to know."

"Your clan cares. Her ancestral bloodline is strong. That will please them. But she has not mingled with the shifter kind. In fact, I'm sure her blood is diluted. It is not known if she can even shift. She might even be human. Her family, that Elvie…" Magda frowned. "Her aunt was known to be flighty. She was best placed exactly where she was in the woods, away from society."

"Rachel is not Elvie, Magda."

"Elvie raised her after she was orphaned." Magda didn't look so sure.

"And she can shift," William told her.

"Oh? Into?" Magda prompted.

William hesitated, unwilling to break Rachel's confidence and feeling only slightly less guilty about lying to Magda. "I believe she is a trout or something like that?"

"Fish?" Magda arched a brow and gave a small shiver. She refused to say more, but her lack of comment spoke volumes. "I have your car ready. There are instructions in the case. The driver doesn't know where he's taking you."

"We're to go into hiding?" William glanced back towards the plane. "Have you told the Duncanis?"

"Trust the Duncanis with a secret? No. Let them worry about their own. Send the Duncanis chief away if you like, but I will not advise you to involve his clan. For all we know, it is his people who hired the mountain lion to come after you."

"You still don't know?" William asked in surprise. "You have had three days to look into it."

That should have been two and a half days longer than the old shifter needed to discover the plot. Magda frowned.

"I'm teasing you," he said to lighten the full force of his shock.

Her frown deepened. "She looks…rough."

William felt Rachel before he saw her. The woman stepped onto the private runway, shading her eyes from the sun. "She is recovering from her injuries. They were severe and we did not have time to let her run. Once we're in the forest, she should be able to heal herself."

"Hm." Magda did not look convinced. "Don't you mean swim?"

"I'll be in touch," William said, turning to go. Part of him had hoped for Magda's blessing, or a kind word, but he was not surprised by the cold reception towards the American shifter.

"Not before you are safe to do so," Magda ordered. She pointed meaningfully at the brief-case. No doubt it was full of specific instructions that he would not exactly follow.

TWELVE

Douglas watched the trees passing by the limo window. He didn't like being out of control, but William was insistent that this place would be safe. Hearing a soft sigh, he glanced at William. The man stared at a file pulled from the briefcase Magda had given him.

"What?" Douglas asked. At the sound of his voice, Rachel looked at William's lap. William handed the file to Douglas. Taking it, he discovered a bridal prospectus of eligible women in Europe. It was written in the old language.

"What is that?" Rachel asked, frowning as if she stared hard enough at the words, she'd suddenly understand them.

"Clan concerns," Douglas said. It wasn't exactly a lie. Everyone was concerned with the future mate of the chiefs. For some reason, he didn't want to tell her that.

"Does this have something to do with the fire?" she asked.

"No." William reached for the file. "Some people wish for us to find a wife in Europe. This is a list of candidates."

Douglas cringed.

"Wife?" Rachel asked. "You're getting married?"

"Of course," William said. "We both are. It is our duty to choose a chieftess."

"So you're not engaged, though, are you?" She seemed to pull back from them.

"Not yet," William said.

"And you?" She looked at Douglas. Her eyes were slightly rounded, the pupils large. He wanted to kiss the expression off her face. Actually, he wanted to throw the inept, young chief out of the moving car and then kiss the expression off her face. He swallowed his jealousy, knowing that he'd have to get over it soon. A very male part of him wanted Rachel to choose him above all others, but he didn't live in a fairytale world where a man and woman got a monogamous happily-ever-after. No, his world demanded sacrifices of him. All he could hope for, all he could ask for was to be one of the two loves of her life. To have otherwise would be to set the clans at war. He would not rip his world apart because he couldn't share.

"We will marry the same woman," William said, clearly surprised. "Don't you know of our ways?"

Rachel looked blankly from one to another.

"The two chiefs must share a bride," Douglas explained. He glanced towards the front divider, listening briefly to the singing driver. Somehow hearing a big, beefy lion shifter's rendition of a teenage pop song was disconcerting. He turned his attention back to Rachel. "It has been our way since the old clan battles. One bride to two chiefs. She is the intermediary between the clans."

"And children?" she inquired.

"The oldest goes to the oldest chief to be raised in the traditions of that clan," Douglas explained. "The second child to the youngest chief, back and forth, repeating until there are no more children."

"Wait." Rachel glanced between the two men. "That would make you two…"

It was easy to see what she what thinking— that two brothers had been in the same bed as her.

"No," William said. "I was adopted. We are not bound by blood."

She sighed with relief. "Good, because that was going to be a little much for me."

"What happened between us is not the usual custom," Douglas said. "It would be best if we did not speak of it."

"Agreed," William said.

"All right." Rachel was more hesitant. "I don't know who'd be asking."

He shared a look with William. Almost any shifter in their kingdoms would like to hear the gossip Rachel could tell.

"Oh, you mean when you marry." She turned her attention to the window, looking a little too hard at the distance. Her expression was stiff and her tone dropped. "I won't say anything about our time together."

"We live our lives under a lot of scrutiny," Douglas said. "It's not like when we were in America. Here, people watch us more closely. They might try to get information out of you if they find you've been in our company."

"I understand," she said.

"We can never give the others reason to doubt us," William added. "If they think we are weak, that we can't uphold our customs, they will demand not only our throne, but our blood. It is not an easy life."

"I said I under—" Her words were cut off by

the sound of squealing tires. The car skidded, throwing them to the side. Douglas slammed into the window. Rachel fell into his ribs, accidently bruising them with the driving force of her elbow. He automatically wrapped his arms around her, trying to hold her tight. The driver jerked the wheel and they flew into the other direction. The sound of breaking glass and bending metal clashed with the roar of an engine. Bodies were thrown around the inside of the car. Douglas didn't let go.

THIRTEEN

RACHEL GROANED, OPENING HER EYES. THE CAR had stopped scraping over the pavement. She pushed against the door, hearing the crunch of glass beneath her stinging palms. The hard road was beneath her, pressed tight to the overturned limo. Shattered crystal glasses and bottles were strewn around her, wetting her bloody hands with the painfully stinging throb of liquor. Douglas lay unconscious in a crumpled heap of limbs. William was gone.

"Help!" Rachel croaked, reaching to untangle herself so she could check on Douglas. A drop of blood fell across his pale cheek and she looked up. William leaned over, reaching down his hand. Crimson trails ran over the side of his face, dripping from the deep gash in his head.

"Rachel? Are you—?"

"William, he's not moving. Help me. I smell gasoline." She hoisted Douglas's body up the best she could. William grabbed Douglas beneath his arms and pulled him out of the vehicle. When William again appeared to help her out, she said, "He was trying to protect me."

"Of course he was," William answered, as if such a thing would be common knowledge.

She grabbed his hand, jumping up as he pulled. She leapt out of the window to land on the car door. Pain racked her and she cradled her ribs. Standing, she looked around the forest. Douglas lay on the ground, unmoving but breathing. She focused on his neck, seeing the gentle beat of his pulse. Smoke trailed from the dented hood of a green pickup several yards behind them. The instincts of the wolf surged within her. She crouched down, turning her attention to the trees.

"Running," she said, pointing into the woods. "There. Two on four legs."

"I hear them," William answered, breathing hard. She heard the shift in his voice.

"Driver?"

"He's dead," William said. "Shot."

"You?"

"I was thrown from the car. I'll live."

"Douglas?"

"Will live."

Rachel felt her body start to shift. She let the anger consume her. "Chase."

"No. Not now. We must get Douglas to safety."

She growled, but resisted the urge to track their attackers. When she looked at William, his silver-filled eyes were just as hungry as hers. They were both breathing hard, as they fought their primal urges. Concern for Douglas finally broke through the animal and drew her attention back to the moment. As if a cloud lifted from her mind, she began to tremble. She leapt from the car, landing next to Douglas. She touched his head.

"They shot our engine," William said. Rachel didn't remember hearing gunfire during the crash. "I'll check the truck. See if you can wake him."

"Douglas?" she asked, stroking his face. He lay on the side of the dirt road. It couldn't have been comfortable, but she wasn't sure if she should move him. "Can you hear me? Open your eyes and look at me."

The truck engine tried to turn over, struggling and sputtering each time William turned the key.

"Dougl—" Rachel tilted her head, listening to the distance. The feet had turned. The attackers were circling back. "William!"

"I hear them. Stay with him. I'll go. We don't know who we're up against."

"No. You stay." Rachel shot to her feet and took off running. She ignored the pain, knowing it would be temporary. "I'm faster."

"Rachel, stop!"

She didn't stop. Spreading her arms, she leapt into the air. Her clothes fell away and feathers sprouted all over her body. She flapped her wings, soaring into the sky. The soreness from the crash melted away with the shift. Trees blurred beneath her as she followed the sound of running feet. A flash of fur revealed the mountain lion, St. Joan. Douglas had called her an "American claw for hire". What was the mercenary doing in the UK? And why was she trying so hard to kill them? Was it as Douglas had implied? Was it because they were two chiefs and some wanted them dead for political reasons? Then why the great lengths to keep her with them? If they were the ones in danger, and both chiefs wished to see her safe as they claimed, then why did they keep her in harm's way? She wasn't stupid. For whatever reason, whether it was association or simple bad luck, she had become a target too. Their three fates were intertwined.

Another blur caught her attention. William

had shifted and ran towards danger, undoubtedly wanting to rescue her before she did anything stupid. She hesitated and lost a little bit of her control. Should she go back to Douglas or help William? Rachel began to descend. She was losing energy and wouldn't be able to maintain the falcon form for long.

Deciding to go where she saw the immediate danger, she circled down. She landed hard, tumbling over herself. Feathers flew around her like lost hairs as she transformed to human. Then, not bothering to lift off the ground, she rolled the other direction, coming to her hands and feet as she shifted into a wolf. With a growl, she burst forward, running through the forest. She heard a wolf's growl and ran faster to heed William's call. The mountain lion answered with a strange, screechy cry, like a demon child calling out for its mother. It sent chills over Rachel's flesh.

Rachel dug her paws into the earth, pushing harder, running faster. As she came upon the brawl, William faced St. Joan and the male leopard beside her. She breathed hard, but the sound of it only excited her already frayed nerves. She wanted to fight, protect, scar. The mountain lion had destroyed her childhood home, the only place she'd felt truly loved and protected. Now the she-bitch was coming after Douglas and William, the two men she…

Well, she couldn't say she loved them, but they did make her feel protected. And she felt a connection to them, a deep, strong, almost feverish connection. Perhaps it was because they were going through something traumatic together. Maybe it was because they were the first shifter boyfriends she'd ever had, the first multiple boyfriends she'd ever had. Or maybe she would feel connected to them no matter the circumstances.

Now was not the time for such contemplation.

The leopard tried to turn as William got in his way. Growling, Rachel lunged, her teeth bared. She landed close to him, forcing him to turn back. St. Joan screeched, slashing her claws defensively seconds before the true brawl began.

Rachel didn't think, didn't hesitate, not like last time when she faced St. Joan and got a claw to the face. Everything she needed to know about fighting was in her blood. She merely reacted. A claw slashed, she ducked. Teeth snarled, she lunged for the soft tissue of a neck. Bite. Growl. Hiss. Claw. There was no order to the chaos. Rachel snapped at the mountain lion before turning her attentions to the leopard. Her teeth hit flesh. Blood filled her mouth, dripping over her chin and neck. The cat yelped and wriggled free, but the gesture only tore the flesh at his own throat. At the sound, William turned his attention to help Rachel. The cat made a gurgling noise as William bit the leopard's back leg and dragged him away from Rachel. St. Joan darted off into the forest.

As if perceiving William as a bigger threat, or perhaps simply a bigger target, the leopard turned his attention around to the man. William held back, giving the man time to run. Rachel was impressed by his restraint, even as she wondered at it. The leopard charged. Rachel leapt, intent on stopping the leopard's attack. William growled defensively, going for the cat's throat. His action blocked Rachel and she fell hard against him. It was over in seconds.

When he pulled away, blood trailed down William's chin. The cat looked stunned before limping off in the direction St. Joan had disappeared. Rachel tensed, tempted to go after him. The smell of blood filled her head, calling to the predator inside her. However, there was no need to give chase. The leopard didn't make it far before dropping to the ground. She stood, tense and ready, but within seconds, the shifter was dead.

Hearing a rustling next to her, she looked at

the other wolf. William pawed the ground, lifting his head. He wanted her to follow him. She nodded. They ran back towards the wreckage. As she thought of Douglas, she grew worried. They'd left him alone. The forest passed in a blur, resounding with the beat of their paws. It didn't take too long before they were by the wrecked vehicles.

William began to shift mid stride, standing on two feet by the time he reached the spot Douglas has been. Muscles rippled over his tight, naked flesh. The red blood from the cat shifter marred his chest and neck. The long line of his spine indented his back, forming a trail down to his firm ass.

Rachel glanced over the area, sensing her surroundings before shifting to human form. She shivered, aware that she stood in the forest naked.

"You're an omni-shifter. Why didn't you say?" William asked, as if the question had been burning inside him.

"Where is he?" Rachel demanded, looking around the area. Her heart pounded in worry as she found her clothing on the ground. She held it against her naked body. "Where is Douglas? You should not have left him alone."

"I didn't have a choice. You flew off." William

walked towards the old truck. "He's in the back. He'll be fine. I kept an ear on him as we fought." Looking in the back, he gestured to where Douglas slept. "See. Already the wounds heal."

The clothes slipped from her fingers, falling to the ground. It might have been the adrenaline of the fight, or the wreck, or even the run through the forest, but she felt her blood hammering in her veins. She touched William's hip. He was so warm. At her caress, he turned narrowed eyes at her.

Before she realized it, she was leaning into him, brushing her lips against his shoulder. He tensed seconds before she felt him give in to her. William made a small sound of pleasure, instantly turning her to press her back into the side of the truck. His cock was in her hand, hard and ready. Moisture flooded her sex, her body just as eager. She stroked him, and he made a small noise of approval.

The urgency of the situation built between them, as if they both knew this was the last thing they should be doing at the moment, and yet they were unable to stop themselves. Rachel told herself they would just find a fast release before moving on.

The mindless euphoria as they touched filled

her. Her hands answered the silent call of his body, running over flexing muscles. He dipped his hand between her thighs, parting her sex. She groaned, rocking into him, desperate for the release he could give.

Rachel nipped at his chest and shoulder, tasting the salt of his flesh and the blood of battle against her tongue. He groaned as she bit him, his muscles tensing beneath her lips. William reached for her ass and lifted her up off the ground as he pressed her tight to the truck for support.

She knew his movements would be raw and primitive, as wild as the wolf inside of him. Rachel craved the hard, primal, pounding love-making. His large cock brushed her slit and she cried out. William thrust, taking her with wild abandon. Her naked breasts bobbed, and he seemed to get much pleasure from watching them.

Clawing his shoulders, she held on. The pleasure built. William breathed hard. His features were pulled tight, as if he fought the beast inside him for control. He slid in and out and in, repeating the violent rhythm until she couldn't keep her eyes open.

She came, her body quivering, her heart thumping, her thighs and stomach burning. The climax rippled through her, causing her to cry out. William thrust deep, jerking his release.

"We should go," William said, his breath catching, even before the tremors subsided fully.

Rachel nodded. "You drive. I'll ride in the back with Douglas and make sure he doesn't move around too much." She began to dress. "Give me your shirt for his head and try to drive easy."

FOURTEEN

RACHEL FLEXED HER ARM, TRYING TO GET THE blood flowing to her tingling hand. She had no idea where they were going or how long it would take. Douglas's head rested across her arm, but she refused to move it. The truck bounced along the road. Her arm and William's thin shirt were the only things padding Douglas's skull from the hard metal bed beneath them.

"You're going to be fine," Rachel whispered in his ear. She brushed a lock of hair off his forehead. The gesture was pointless as the wind only blew it back. "I can see the cuts on your face already starting to heal. It won't be long now."

He didn't answer. She knew her words were pointlessly spoken, only meant to comfort herself in her worry. His body might heal itself, but the brain would not. If he suffered from brain damage, he might not recover or even wake up. Shifter powers could only do so much.

"Thank you for shielding me from the wreck," she continued, again brushing back the hair only to have the wind push it across his forehead once more. "I—" The truck slowed, and they slid a little towards the front of the truck bed. She grunted in discomfort. "I promise I'll stay with you until you're awake and able to take care of yourself. I'll take care of you as you took care of me. St. Joan won't get her paws on you."

Rachel wasn't sure what prompted the oath, but she didn't want to take it back. The truck continued to slow its progression. Unable to see, she finally pulled her arm out from under Douglas's head and sat up. William pulled into a long cobblestone drive in front of an English country estate. When he said they were going to hide out, she didn't expect it would be in some sort of nineteenth century nobleman's mansion.

A nervous knot formed in her stomach. The yard looked lush and green, trimmed perfectly, as if the gardener stood outside all day with a ruler just to make sure. Small stone trails sprouted off the cobblestone drive, winding around the home before breaking off in several directions into a garden before ultimately disappearing into an area encased by stone walls.

The house itself spread wide across the land-scape and looked as if it could hold fifty of her aunt's cabins. She wondered how many people lived inside the towering walls. A wide, oak door opened, and a couple servants stepped out followed by the woman Rachel had seen at the airport. She didn't look happy. Remembering that the woman had given William a list of prospective brides, Rachel frowned. By the look on Douglas's face as William had mentioned it in the car, she knew her name wasn't on the list. Why should it be? Didn't royalty have to marry aristocrats, or power animals? Yes, she was powerful, but her two lovers were the only ones with any idea as to her abilities.

The servants moved cautiously down the round sweep of steps leading from the front door. William pulled to a stop, and the two women visibly relaxed as they saw who was driving the beat-up vehicle. The older woman moved forward in front of the others, but didn't deign to move closer. Her lips pursed tightly together.

"Magda," William said. "The Duncanis chief is injured. We must get him inside. Fetch help."

The older woman, whose name was evidently Magda, disappeared inside to do as her chief commanded. The maids approached the back of the truck, straining to see inside where Douglas was. Then, their curiosity somewhat sated, they turned harder gazes to Rachel. She narrowed her eyes at them, too sore and too tired to deal with whatever was going on in their heads. As a big brute of a man passed between them, the maids backed away, scurrying up the steps.

"Douglas," Rachel whispered, trying to get him to wake up. For a moment, she thought she heard him groan, but any future sound was muffled by the clang of the opening truck bed. William appeared next to the brute and they both reached in to pull Douglas into their arms so they could carry him inside.

"Duncanis," Magda muttered in contempt, as if the single word conveyed all the weakness and unworthiness of Douglas's unconscious form.

"He saved my life," Rachel snapped, not liking the woman's tone.

Magda's sharp eyes turned to Rachel, sweeping up and down. The woman evidently didn't think much of Douglas's heroic deed. Apparently, Rachel wasn't worth saving.

"This way," Magda ordered, turning her back on Rachel. "I'll take you around to the servants' entrance and show you were you can wash that wildness off of you."

"Rachel," William called as they hauled Douglas inside, "this way."

Rachel, unable to help herself, gave Magda a superior look. She went towards the front door. "Coming!"

❖

"I DON'T THINK MAGDA APPROVES OF ME," Rachel said to William, as she studied Douglas on the bed. The servants had removed his shirt, and she'd been shocked to see the massive purpling over the man's chest. A bandage wrapped his ribs, a stark white to his tanned flesh. Their kind normally could heal from such rib wounds, but that didn't mean he was out of the woods yet, nor did it mean he wasn't in pain.

"She's just set in her ways and likes things the way she likes them." William dismissed the concern. "She has a lot to contend with and is worried about us being here and possibly in harm's way. The plan was to hide out until it could be discovered who was after us. Though secure, if someone at court wants to do us harm, this mansion isn't the safest place. Too many people are coming and going."

"Worried about *you* maybe," Rachel said. William didn't answer.

"We should go get something to eat. There is not much we can do for Douglas but let him rest. I will have someone come and check on him."

Rachel made a move to crawl onto the bed. "You go ahead. I'm sure you have business to attend to. I'll stay here with Douglas." Without thinking about it, she stretched out on the mattress.

William hesitated, as if he would protest. Then, slowly he nodded. He gestured to a velvet rope hanging near the wall. "Ring if you need anything. I'll be back later to check on you both." He hesitated again before finally leaving.

Rachel curled next to Douglas, running her hand lightly over his chest. "Hey, you need to wake up. I'm not sure we're safe here. I didn't like how some of the people were looking at us. William doesn't want to hear it because this is a Cononious mansion, but there was something not right with that Magda woman." She gently pulled on a bandage, lifting it to peek under. His ribs were still bruised. "Douglas?"

"Uh," he groaned, turning his head back and forth on the pillow before finally settling his gaze on her.

She sighed with relief. "You're awake."

"You smell pretty," he murmured.

Rachel laughed. "I think you might have hit your head. How are you feeling?"

"Like I was in a car wreck."

"That would be a fitting conclusion. You've been out a long time." She rested her hand low on his stomach, propping herself on her elbow to study his face. "We're at the Cononious mansion. William just left."

"I recognize the room."

Rachel quickly told him everything that had happened, leaving out the part where she and William had sex against the side of the truck in an explosion of after-battle release. If he asked her, she wouldn't lie, but she saw no reason to bring it up.

"You're an omni-shifter?" He arched a brow. Other than that, he didn't make any quick movements.

Rachel nodded. "Yes."

"How many?"

There was no point in lying about it now.

"Falcon, wolf, shark. Wolf is the strongest and most natural for me. I can't seem to hold on to the falcon form too long, and I don't really have call to use the shark. The few times I have, I tend to get mindlessly lost in the ocean. By the time I've adjusted enough to shift back, I have no idea where I'm at." Rachel tried to act as if it wasn't a big deal. "I'm too scared I will get lost at sea. There's something about the ocean that calls you out of your head."

"Air, land, and sea," Douglas said. His hand skimmed over the top of hers, holding it to his lower stomach. Covers lay across his waist, hiding his hips from view. "I don't think you know how rare a gift the omni-shift is. In my father's time, he had scientists working to discover why certain people were omni-shifters, or wolves, or birds, or even fish. They were trying to unlock the genetic key."

"Elvie told me stories of such experiments," Rachel answered. Her stomach tensed, but for some reason she sensed she could trust him, just as she could trust William. "She said if anyone found out about me, they might take me away and do experiments on me. That is why I tell people I am a trout. It's safer and easier that way."

"No one would dare to harm you, but would merely honor you for your gifts. I stopped the experiments years ago."

She frowned. It wasn't a denial that such things had happened in the past.

"But we will keep your secret," he said. "If that is what you wish."

The feel of silken covers brushed her finger, and she realized he'd inched her hand lower on his stomach. She glanced down his body, seeing the unmistakable lift of an erection beneath the cream-colored silk. "Are you feeling better?"

"Somewhat." His breathing deepened. "I can think of something that would make me feel even better."

"That has to be the worst pick-up line in history." She let him slide her hand lower and her fingers became tangled in silk.

"But it's working, isn't it?" He gave a small laugh. "Please say it is working."

"You could have tried a little harder, but considering you took a window to the back for me, I guess I can overlook it."

"Then my plan worked." He laughed harder, bringing her fingers to rest over his arousal. His bold confidence excited her. "You're in my debt."

He made an effort to sit up, but she removed her hand from his cock and pressed his shoulder to keep him down. "You should take it easy. Some of your ribs might be broken. I almost demanded they take you to an emergency room, but—"

He shook his head in denial. "I'm hardly a frail human. There is a Cononious doctor in the mansion should the need ever arise. If memory serves, he'll be dead drunk in a bedroom in the east wing. We have little need of his services and he enjoys a life at court."

"I clearly went into the wrong profession," Rachel said, giving a meaningful look around their lush surroundings. "I could have been living it up as a posh doctor to patients who never needed me."

"Wouldn't it be much better to be treated like a queen than a servant?" Douglas brushed back her hair.

Rachel chuckled. Being treated like a queen didn't sound so bad. "Well, my chief, why don't you relax? Let me play doctor and see how I like it."

"You're hired. Come away with me to my court at once."

"I haven't even started my audition yet."

She moved to kneel beside him, leaning over his stomach. She ran her hands over his body, careful not to touch his wounded ribs as she massaged his hips and thighs through the silk. Taking her time, she rubbed his legs, letting the silk make an agonizingly slow trip down his body, unveiling tight hips and firm flesh like a curtain lifting over a grand stage. She scratched nails lightly over his exposed length.

She kissed a trail down his magnificent form, starting at the edge of his bandage and moving across the sensitive flesh of his hip. She nipped him with her teeth and his body contracted. He began to sit up and she paused until he settled back down.

The tips of his fingers brushed against her cheek, tangling in the locks of her hair. She wanted him. She felt it as surely as she felt anything. But then she also wanted William. Confusion filled her. She'd tried for so long to be like the full-blooded humans, but she was not human, not completely. Humanity and the beast warred within her, they always warred, but here she was free to let a little of the beast roam free— or in her case beasts. She felt more than heard the shifters around her, filling up the large estate. It was a wild energy that pulsed through the walls, as uncontainable as the beasts that caused it.

Douglas encouraged her mouth to move downward, and her conflicted thoughts were momentarily lost in the taste of his skin. He smelled clean, a tinge of soap and natural musk. She moved silk over his legs, inch by inch, kissing the exposed thigh, then knee, then calf, before lifting it away from his flesh. His feet stirred as she made her way back up. She didn't close her eyes, instead watching the erotic shifts of muscles beneath her.

Taking his balls, she rolled them in her palm. Her lips brushed over the tip of his shaft, teasing it with tiny licks. He moaned, before tensing and holding his breath. She worked her mouth over him, taking in his thick length.

Desire rippled through her, washing over her entire body in waves. She couldn't get enough of him. Douglas gasped. He jerked, pulling her off him before his seed spilled. He lifted her by the shoulders, bringing her mouth up to his. She made a weak noise of protest, but his kiss silenced her.

He rolled onto his side, pinning her against him. His leg slipped over hers, holding them down. "You are a miracle worker. I feel much better already."

Fingers peeled at the layers of clothing that kept her flesh from his hands. Silver flashed in his eyes and he crawled over her with a predatory grace. His lips brushed across her breasts, teasing the peaks before they passed lower. He gave her body the same attention she'd given his, only his caresses were harder, sucking and licking and biting down and up her legs.

Rachel writhed beneath him, spreading her legs as he neared her sex. Her pussy was wet, ready for his touch. She felt no inhibitions when she was with him. When Douglas caressed her, looked at her, moved over her with graceful intent, she knew she was safe. His smoldering gaze told her he wanted her, a deep and burning need that could barely be contained.

He nipped at her inner thigh, instantly soothing the tiny bite with wet kisses. Douglas licked his way towards the apex of her thighs. Warm, firm lips glided along her slit, as he parted the folds of her sex with his tongue. She moaned softly, knowing she should protest and demand he mind his wounds, but the pleasure of his mouth felt too great. Hair tickled her thigh. She watched his head move between her legs.

He stroked her with his tongue, rubbing the tight bud of her clit with the moist, hard pressure of it. She squirmed and threaded her legs over his back to pull him closer. When he growled, the dark sound vibrated her and her hips jerked violently. He did it again, rubbing harder. His nose skimmed the top arch. His tongue swept up and in, only to return to her clit once more. She grabbed his hair, vaguely aware of the incoherent pleas escaping her lips. She ground against him. Tension built, almost painful in its intensity. And then finally, sweet release. She came, jerking and panting, tensing and kicking. It was too much, and she pushed at his shoulders to back his mouth away. She couldn't catch her breath.

Wickedly seductive eyes found hers as he

finally released her clit from his kiss. He crawled over her. "I like you wet."

Before she could protest, the unmistakably hard press of his cock found entrance. He thrust into her pussy, filling her trembling sex with the full length of his staff. Douglas began to strain, fucking her in long, gliding strokes. The smooth pull of muscles drew her eyes to his chest. Red had seeped into the bandages, staining the white with crimson streaks. He didn't seem to notice.

Hips pounded her ass into the mattress. Grabbing a leg, he lifted it over and across his body so that both of her legs lay against one of his hips. The position tightened her pussy's hold on his cock and he groaned. His words came in hard gasps, "Ah, there. Take me. Take it all." He grabbed her wrists, pinning her down. As the pleasure built inside her once more, he found his own release. A subtler, gentler climax hit her the second time, building upon the one she'd just experienced.

With a groan, he fell next to her on the bed. Rachel's heart pounded violently. A smile crossed her features as she straightened her limbs. Then, remembering the red, she turned to Douglas in concern. His eyes were closed and he breathed deeply. Reaching for the bandages, she pulled them back to see his injuries. Though there was blood, she couldn't find any open wounds where it could have come from. The puckered marks which should have seeped were healed shut.

Douglas's hand skated up to cover hers, stopping her exploration of him. He didn't open his eyes. Rachel settled next to him, too drained to move.

FIFTEEN

"DID YOU LOOK AT THAT LIST I GAVE YOU?" Magda asked, taking her place by William.

William turned his attention from where he stared at the ceiling to the old shifter. "No. There is no need. I think we've made our decision."

"The American?" she frowned. "I had hoped once you got to the United States you would see how distasteful the heathens there are. There is a reason they're isolated from the rest of us. They're a wild, dirty lot of half-breeds."

"This isn't the dawn of the American War of Independence, Magda. It's not all peasant colonies and religious outcasts over there." He frowned. Sometimes she was so old-fashioned that he wanted to drag her kicking and screaming into the modern age. Though, to be fair, he doubted Magda knew how to kick and scream. For a shifter she was very well reserved. Strangely though, she was somewhat of a computer genius. He guessed it came from her insatiable desire to be always informed.

"I'm well aware of the year," she quipped. "The only thing worse than an American bride, is an Australian one."

Instead of needlessly informing her that Australia was no longer a prison dumping ground but a thriving continent filled with interesting people, he sighed. "Rachel is special. I think she is up to the task of being queen of the clans." He almost said she was an omni-shifter, but refrained. That one word would have probably quieted the old woman's protests, but he would not betray Rachel's trust. She clearly did not want her gifts to be part of the public record, and that is exactly where Magda would put it. Why else would she claim to be a trout instead of one of the most powerful shifters he'd ever seen?

"Is it settled?"

"Not yet. We have not asked her." William turned his attention back to the ceiling. He knew what Douglas and Rachel were doing. They'd been up there all night. He tried to cool his jealousy, but it unfurled within him. He wanted to be with her. She should be in his bed. She should be in his arms. She should be his.

William was not born into royalty. He did not have the ease that Douglas seemed to carry when it came to sharing the beautiful Rachel. It had only been a short time and already he burned to possess all of her. What would happen when it came to marriage? When the months turned into years turned into decades? Would the jealous feelings lessen? Become some bearable echo he found other ways to ignore? Or would it eat at him, gnawing away at his heart and his sanity until he went crazy with it, feral? Shifters were not meant to share. Not like this.

"William!" Magda said, none too gently. He blinked heavily, looking at her. "This is what I'm talking about. You cannot afford to be distracted, and you cannot show that you are jealous of the other chief. It will be seen as a weakness. You have to be strong. Do you think the Duncanis chief will show such emotion? No. Listen to me. Find a bride, a *lady* that you can control yourself around. That is the way to be content in your role. You must suppress the beast within."

"Lisbetha you mean." He sighed heavily. The blonde was pretty and knew the aristocratic shifter ways, more so than Rachel. Lisbetha understood the customs and ceremonies. Rachel would have to be taught. William knew the logic in this. But still… He glanced to the ceiling.

"Or Ginger, or Margot, or Fai—"

"For the sake of my ears, please do not name them all again. Chief Douglas does not have such headaches, I am sure of it." William moaned, rubbing his temple. "Let us first concentrate on who hired St. Joan, and then we'll worry about the matter of my future bride."

"She seems small. Are you sure she can give you strong children?" Magda asked in a last effort to dissuade him.

"Magda," William warned, letting the beast into his voice. She instantly changed the subject.

"We assumed that it was someone wanting to stop you from taking an American bride, or someone wanting your throne, but word has come that the vampire king was not pleased at your swift departure and took it as a slight. He has expressed displeasure and his scorn towards you. The goblin queen is irked that she has not gotten a personal invitation to your court."

"I thought the goblins were in hibernation."

"They are, but they will wake up to spread their ill humor." Magda frowned. "And, incidentally, the fairies have put forth bridal candidates for your consideration. I have already graciously declined and reminded them that the last pairing of shifter and fairy did not end well."

"Didn't the shifter...?" William cringed.

"Yes. He tore her asunder during the wedding night. Fairy lust is too potent for the beasts we carry." Then, getting right back on topic, she said, "So, jealous shifters, vampire king, goblin queen, ah, oh yes, and the witches' union."

"The witches' union?" His head throbbed harder. "What slight have I performed against the witches' union?"

"The northern factions are generally discontent with everyone. Their attentions will turn from you in fifty years or so, or when word of another accession reaches their ears. Do not worry. All your food is tested and their hexes rarely take hold over our kind. At worse, you can expect a rash."

William arched a brow, not even wanting to delve into that last comment. Sarcastically, he drawled, "What, no death threats from the chupacabras?"

"No. I think they mostly take their frustrations out on goats and sheep." Magda sighed. "If you are not going to take me seriously because you can't turn your mind from the American, then go get her out of your system. I have a ball to plan."

"A ball?" That got his attention. "I would think you wanted us to lay low."

"I did. I didn't ask you to come here instead of the safe house. But as you're home and with the other chief in tow, it will be expected you show your face in public. Let whoever it is know you will not be intimidated. Security will be tightened."

Normally, William would be all for confronting this issue head first. That was before he had Rachel to think about. He didn't want her in harm's way. This ball was an open invitation to trouble.

"Go," Magda ordered a little too harshly. Her annoyance was clear. "Take your turn at her."

"I had thought that after my accession you would have become a little more respectful," he muttered, pushing to his feet. He couldn't deny he wanted to see Rachel.

"If you want someone to coddle you like a newborn, find a midwife." Magda marched away before he could answer.

Sighing, William made his way up the stairs, turning once he reached the top to go to the wing reserved for the Duncanis chief and his traveling escorts. Though now, only two people occupied the hall.

His stomach tight, he hesitantly listened to the distance. With great relief, he didn't hear sounds of lovemaking coming from Douglas's room. He quickened his pace. A strange rolling noise sounded at the far side of the hall, coming from around a corner. Then, after a crash, the sound of laughter.

William quickened his pace. As he came to the end of the hall, he heard Rachel scream, "Watch out!"

He leapt back as a ball sped past his feet.

Rachel jogged towards him, looking guilty even as she laughed. "Sorry, I didn't hear you coming. We weren't paying attention."

When he glanced past her, he saw a grouping of old wooden bowling pins set up in the hallway. Douglas leaned against the wall, his arms crossed over his chest and an easy smile over his lips. William stepped aside as Rachel hurried past him to get the wooden bowling ball that had almost tripped him.

"Up for a game, ol' chap?" Douglas asked.

"We found the set in a trunk," Rachel said.

"We?" Douglas repeated, arching a brow.

"I found the set in a trunk while snooping through the guest rooms," Rachel corrected. "He was asleep and I was bored."

"You could have found me," William said.

"I'm sure you were busy doing your princely duties. I didn't want to be a bother," she answered.

"She didn't want to face your court," Douglas corrected. Rachel laughed as if the two of them shared a private joke. William tried to swallow down his jealousy, but it would be impossible to miss the ease with which the other two conversed. What happened during the night they spent together?

"That's too bad," William answered, after a long pause. "A ball is being planned in honor of the visiting chief. Apparently, we can't get out of it. It's expected."

"I forgot how much was expected when you're new to the throne." Douglas took the ball and hefted back his arm. Giving it a toss, he paused, watching as the old toy wobbled as it rolled towards the pins at a strange angle. Rachel laughed, hitting Douglas's arm. Douglas's hand slid over hers briefly. The ball managed to hit a couple of the pins.

William felt like an outsider intruding on a couple's private moments. Still, he couldn't force himself to go.

"Well, I think you two will make very handsome dates to the ball," Rachel said.

"So you will come?" William asked, surprised at her easy acceptance.

"Oh no, I meant for each other. You two will make very handsome dates for each other." Rachel lifted her hand to brush her fingers over his forearm. He clenched his fist, feeling a tingle erupt beneath his flesh. "I have no intention of going to a royal ball. In fact, I've been thinking I'd explore the countryside a little, perhaps London. I'm assuming, of course, if I get into trouble for being here without a passport, you'll come rescue me."

"You can't," Douglas said. "It isn't safe."

"That's one of the things I've come to tell you. My people are working on narrowing down who the threat is." William sighed heavily. His arms still tingled where she'd touched him. The beast in him wanted to demand its turn. The man in him held the beast back. He repeated the information he'd gotten from Magda about the possible attackers.

"I'm assuming the fairies have sent you bridal candidates?" Douglas asked. William nodded that they indeed had. "Send them on to the Vampire king with your apology. They will be willing and the offering will appease Kristoff's bloodlust and anger. He has a fiery temper, but he would not hire assassins to do his dirty work. It's a matter of pride with the vampires. The goblin queen is always irked. It is when she is happy that you have to worry. Do not send her the invite or you will have goblins crawling all over your court until the end of time. They are harder to get rid of than an infestation of spirits."

"And the witches?" Rachel asked, her face a little pale.

"Could be a problem. Julianne and Bella, known generally as the 'cursed sisters', have a thing for causing royal trouble. I don't see them hiring assassins, but it's not beyond the realm of possibilities. Anyway, I'm expecting a call from my people. I'll have them check into it. The northern factions have festival grounds about seventy-five miles from my home."

"I think I need to go lie down." Rachel slowly moved down the hall.

"Rachel?" William asked, not liking the worried look on her face.

"I'm just feeling a little out of it. I just found out that not only are there fairies and vampires, but goblins and witches. I'm assuming they're magical witches and not, well…"

"Yes, they do practice the old magic," Douglas answered.

"I guess I spent so much time trying not to act like a shifter, I never stopped to think about what other different things might be out there." Rachel ran her hands through her hair. "So this is really happening. I'm stuck here with a target pasted to my forehead."

"No harm will come to you," William said.

"We promise," Douglas affirmed.

"Until you find a wife. I can't imagine the new chieftess will take kindly to your protecting a mistress," she said, slowly backing from them. "I'm sorry. I need some time alone."

"Don't leave the manor," Douglas said. The words sounded more like an order than a request. Though, to William, much of what Douglas said had a kind of condescension to it, a tone born of his rank and privilege.

Rachel gave a quick salute before turning the corner. William listened to her footsteps. When they faded, he asked, "When should we tell her? I don't want to wait."

"I don't think she's ready to be asked. She seems fairly certain we will choose another." Douglas frowned. "When I tried to take her to breakfast, she insisted we hide out instead. I don't think she's ready for the attention that such a position will bring. I don't think she's ready to admit to our kind that she's one of us. I don't want the idea of a future with us to chase her away."

"A shifter who doesn't want to be a shifter," William said, "and with the power she possesses."

"Perhaps your ball is a good idea. We will introduce her to the court." Douglas leaned over to pick up the pins. "As our future queen, she'll need to get used to the limelight."

SIXTEEN

RACHEL STOPPED, TILTING HER HEAD TO THE side. By the sound of the male voices, it was clear they didn't realize how good her hearing was.

As our future queen, she'll need to get used to the limelight.

Did she hear that correctly? Future queen? From living a private life she loved, to becoming the single, most powerful female shifter on the planet?

A shifter who doesn't want to be a shifter and with the power she possesses.

They wanted her because of her powers. Didn't Elvie warn her never to tell her secret? Then again, they were talking about marrying her, not turning her into an experiment.

"*Marriage?*" she whispered, as the thought fully

hit her. Maybe an experiment would be better than that.

She took a deep breath. They both wanted to marry her. Two husbands. Two *chief* husbands. A small thrill worked through her at the thought of spending her life with William and Douglas. She never expected to want two men. But then reality came crashing around her. What would happen after the fairytale was over? If the fire she felt inside her died? Or their eyes wandered? Shifters generally mated to one person. How exactly did a three-person marriage work for them? Would she bond to one and not the other? The idea of hurting either man didn't sit well with her. What would happen when the honeymoon ended and she was trapped as some celebrity? Every move would be examined, photographed, watched. She'd never be able to run completely free again. Gone would be the wild dashes through the mountains. Could she take such a leap? Could she give up her privacy and her life?

Her eyes wide, she looked around the empty hall. The Elizabethan style was beautiful and old and reminded her of a museum. People weren't supposed to live in museums, at least not in real life—maybe in fiction novels, or epic movies, or in historical dramas, but not real life.

She felt the people around her, filling the halls

and rooms, walking the gardens outside and running just beyond the fences. It was an energy that pulsed, reminding her of her childhood when Elvie's home was surrounded by shifters. There was comfort in the sensation, but also a fear.

Everything was happening too fast. She hadn't known these men long. It was too soon to start thinking about marriage and forever. They were just getting to know each other. They were just having fun. They couldn't really think to make her choose marriage right away, could they?

The reality of her situation came crashing in around her. She was an American in Europe—without ID, without money, without a passport—with an assassin looking to kill her. The few friends she had at work would not have the means to help her out. It wasn't like the US government would listen to a busboy and waitress when it came to matters of citizenship and international travel. If she went to the embassy, they would want to know how she managed to get overseas. There was no record of her travel by commercial flights. The shifters wouldn't be happy with her if she exposed them for a ticket home.

Even so, the thick manor walls seemed to cave in on her and she needed to get out. Hurrying through the hall, she wasn't sure where she was going. She needed to think. She rushed past antique paintings and gilded mirrors. Finally, feeling a slight breeze, she followed it to the source —a window at the end of a long hall. Making her way to it, she pushed it open and jumped down to the cobblestone below. A perfectly manicured garden made it easy to hide as she ducked behind long stretches of shrubbery and trees. She smelled the woods before she saw them. The dense tree line called to her and she ran, letting the power of the shift come over her limbs. Her clothes fell away as she hit the ground on all fours. Freedom.

SEVENTEEN

WILLIAM GROWLED IN FRUSTRATION. THE moment Magda had informed him of Rachel's run in the private forest, he'd gone after her. Though part of his property, the forest wasn't exactly the most protected. As shifters, they tended to feel a sense of security when it came to intruders. Though, to be fair, normally there wasn't an assassin after them.

He dropped his clothing outside the manor's door and hit the ground running, well aware that the eyes of his court might be on him. He didn't care. He needed to find Rachel. This wasn't the American wild where she grew up, where shifters were more relaxed and tended to mind their own business. Here, there were certain expected behaviors, and it was already clear no one had bothered to school Rachel on just what those etiquettes were. One was that unattached ladies didn't run the forest alone—unless they were looking to get caught.

Okay, so that rule was antiquated, but when it came to his future bride, he found it fairly sound. If he had his way, she'd be put under lock and key and constant supervision.

So that was extreme. He knew it and still he felt the desire to do it.

The forest became a blur as he headed towards the main path. He had run through these woods thousands of times and could navigate the darkening trails with ease. The familiar smells filled him, guiding him as easily as his sight. Rachel's scent was faint, almost buried beneath the other more powerful ones.

His heart beat a steady rhythm in his chest, keeping time with his drumming feet. Her scent became stronger, driving him on. He turned west, heading deeper into the trees. Then, another smell wafted over him like a death omen. It was the acrid scent of blood, freshly spilt.

The beast within him raged, becoming mindless as he surged forward, leaping over fallen trunks as he cut through the denser trees. He became aware of someone following him and assumed Magda told Douglas what had happened. No doubt the other chief smelled the blood as well and came to investigate.

His feet slid to a stop as the scent grew stronger. The sound of it dripped in a steady rhythm on the leafy ground. He narrowed his eyes, piercing the darkened forest with his shifted gaze. Then he saw her. Rachel was bound to a tree in human form. Blood ran down her arm from a deep gash, trailing crimson on her naked flesh as it flowed to the ground. Dazed eyes found his, her lids heavy. She moaned against a gag in her mouth, the incoherent syllables more of an expression of pain than a call for help.

His fur stood on end as he slowed his approach. Scanning the forest, he didn't detect movement in the trees. What was this? A warning?

Rachel moaned again and his attention focused on her. He neared her and extended a paw. The rope cord loosened when he hooked his foot into a loop and pulled.

The sound of footsteps became louder. William turned, intent on acknowledging Douglas. Only then did he notice the forest smell was off. It wasn't Douglas who came after him. He'd been so focused on Rachel that he didn't stop to think things out completely. A naked woman stood, chest heaving, black hair tousled around her shoulders, dark eyes filled with victory. She held a gun pointed at his head.

"Hello, chief," she said, smiling. "Don't bother standing up. You'll do just fine like that."

William growled, but there was nothing he could do. She pulled the trigger. White-hot fire pierced his neck, and though he tried to stay on his feet, he felt his legs giving out. He fell hard on the ground, striking his head against the earth seconds before his world turned black.

EIGHTEEN

"What do you mean they're gone?" Douglas demanded. His eyes narrowed on Magda. His clan had dealt with her often over the years and, though she was highly capable at her job as the chief's glorified secretary, she was an elitist pain in their ass. For some reason, she'd gotten it in her head that her clan was superior in all things. Such egotism wasn't unusual with hot-blooded shifters. Daring to show it so openly to the opposing chief was.

"My chief went after the American in the forest. She ran away from the manor without an escort." Magda's expression gave nothing away, but Douglas read the irritation clearly in her eyes. "That was two hours ago. I assumed they were," she paused, "otherwise engaged in the woods. But he has yet to come back. I thought I should inform you that I have sent the guards in to investigate the situation and have increased the security on the grounds."

"Two hours?" Douglas repeated, barely hearing the rest. "Why was I not informed before now?"

"I do not work for you, Duncanis." Magda's jaw snapped shut and she refused to look him in the eye. "It was not my duty to report on my chief to you."

"You should have told me. You know what this woman means. I'm going after them."

His heart beat hard inside his chest, each painful thump an echo of his worry.

"We have—" she began.

"I am going after them!" He didn't wait for her to respond as he brushed past her towards the front door. He hurried down the steps to the cobblestone walkway leading around the side of the house. Not caring what kind of scene he made, he tore at his clothes, ripping them from his body as he made his way over the thick lawn. He leapt, shifting midair before running into the forest on all fours. He darted through the trees in a haphazard pattern as he tried to pick up Rachel's scent. Each second caused his stomach to knot all the more. He growled, hoping someone would hear him, answer him. It wasn't to be. Minutes later he found a trace of her in the blood-tinged ground.

Shifting, he stood naked in the forest—his body tense, his heart pounding, his temple throbbing. He was too late. William and Rachel were gone.

❧

RACHEL BLINKED, HER LIDS HEAVY. HER HEAD rolled back and forth, pressing into the hard concrete wall that supported her head. When she lifted her arms, they felt as if they were filled with liquid steel and not blood. Her thoughts were suspended between awake and sleep, making it hard to concentrate. Whatever St. Joan had given her had knocked her out like a thousand milligrams of the strongest prescription sedative.

Realization came slowly. First it was the drip, drip, drip of water on stone. Next, the hard ground littered with pebbles that seemed to find each and every nerve ending along the backs of her thighs and ass. Then, the cold—not so bitter as to be unbearable, but chilly enough to be uncomfortable. Finally, the smell. She coughed, her lungs automatically trying to expel the scent from her body. The rank odor of decay and death filled her mouth as she gasped for air, leaving it with a bad taste.

Rachel blinked again, trying to clear the fog clouding her mind. But it wasn't her shut lids that kept her from seeing. Her prison was as black as a grave. By the smell, she assumed the assessment wasn't that far off. From a solitary life in America to being held prisoner in an English cemetery.

"What the hell am I doing?" She forced her brain to concentrate as she steeled her nerves. "Now is not the time to dwell. I am here and I need to find a way out."

By sheer willpower she managed to push off the ground, awkwardly rolling from her back to rest first on her elbows, then finally up on her hands. She tried to pierce the darkness, but could only make out the faint outline of shapes, giant blocks and curves, walls and ceilings.

"Find a way out," she repeated, this time like a command. Raising her hand over her head, she stood, reaching towards the ceiling. When her head didn't hit anything, she reached to the side, sweeping her fingers back and forth as she inched first one way, then another. "Find a way out, Rachel. She put you in, you can get out."

NINETEEN

THREE DAYS.

Douglas felt like he hadn't been able to breathe for three very long days. That's how long it had been since he'd found out Rachel and William were missing, since he'd smelled her blood on the ground. Blood. Not a lot of it, but blood nonetheless. Logic told him that she'd heal from such a wound, but what if they injured her more? There was no ransom, not even for Chief William. If they didn't want money, then…

The traitors had already tried to kill them.

Douglas growled, grabbing his head. He ran his fingers into his hair, pulling hard. His body yearned for sleep, but his mind wouldn't shut off. How could it? She was out there. Every part of him wanted her, yearned to hold her close. He never thought he'd feel so much for a woman. Other shifters had the luxury of a single mate, but his lot was different. He always thought there would be a part of him that would be held back from women, a part that wouldn't connect, a part that would be able to let go.

Unlike humans, his kind didn't need months or years to know they were in love. They trusted themselves more, trusted their instincts, and every instinct inside him was telling him to grab his woman and lock her away from the big, bad world. Only he couldn't find his woman.

"Chief Douglas." The purring sound of Lisbetha's voice came from behind. The woman had a grace to her actions and a softness to her words. Douglas frowned. It was an irritating grace and softness, so persistently nice and calm, always lurking a few steps behind him. "Magda sent me to find you. She's worried that you haven't eaten since you've come back to the manor this afternoon."

"I doubt she's worried," Douglas said under his breath.

"Very well. Then I'm worried." Lisbetha touched his arm. "People are beginning to wonder at your mood."

Douglas frowned. His moods were no concern of hers, and it was presumptuous of her to even mention it. He glanced at where she touched him, intent on telling her as much, but her wide eyes found his and he hesitated. The clear depths looked so sweet, so earnest, he couldn't yell at her. Instead, he shrugged off her touch under the pretense of turning. "I am going to search the forest again with my men."

"But," Lisbetha said softly behind him. He ignored her. She yelled, "But you've been out there every day for the last four days! Stay inside. Let me tend to you. Nothing can be done right now."

Douglas stopped. Four days? He looked at his hand, ticking off the days on his fingers. She was right. Four days, not three.

Lisbetha's footsteps crept up behind him. He walked faster, leaving her to stare after him.

Four days.

TWENTY

"ALMOST TIME, CHIEF," ST. JOAN WHISPERED, smiling at the man tied before her.

William growled, half drugged by powerful sedatives. Tiny trails of blood lined his naked body, but the wounds beneath them had healed. They were meant to torture, to keep his body weak. The drugs kept him lucid enough to understand, but dazed enough not to fight back too hard. His shoulder hurt from where he hung off the ground. His arms had been stretched to the sides, suspending him off the earth. The ropes that held him were wrapped around two thick trees. He had tried to free himself, but the swinging motion threatened to pull his arms out of his shoulder sockets.

St. Joan's dark eyes reminded him of a feral

cat. There was a wildness in them not seen in tamer animals. Though graceful, her body jerked and stiffened at any sudden noise in the distance. She tried to hide the reaction, but some things were so innate they couldn't be helped. The woman had not been raised in society. He pictured her roaming the American wilderness, living in the backwoods somewhere as a dirt-covered child. He'd seen her type before—reclusive, inelegant, socially awkward, yet dangerous and lethal. The instincts of the animal had been fed within her, but the human part of her had been neglected to the point it was now only a shadow of the mountain lion inside. It was what made her a perfect claw for hire. She would not be loyal to her clan, but to herself and to a very limited point, her employer.

"Twice you got in my way," she continued, pacing like a caged animal. Her dark hair flew unhampered about her shoulders, uncombed. She didn't even register her own nakedness as she moved. "Three, if you count Bert, but I don't. The leopard was a good fighter. Stupid but loyal. It will be hard to replace him. Very inconvenient."

"Twice?" William mumbled. He tried to concentrate, tried to remember that he needed to know who hired her. It was difficult, but he managed by staring at her mouth for the words.

"I was sent to burn the bitch," St. Joan said. "You stopped me. I don't get paid if I get stopped."

"Who?" he managed.

St. Joan laughed. "No, no, no, Chief, not that."

"Why?"

She laughed harder. "Who cares? I was offered a lot of money to go to Colorado, track and kill the shifter bitch, and to take out anyone who got in my way. It was a beautiful fire, was it not? I was so excited to see my target owned the sanctuary. So much wood and leaves and kindling. I had hoped it would spread across the countryside like my last forest fire, but the explosion when the generator went was glorious."

"Rachel was your target?" Fear consumed him. Why did someone want Rachel dead? Was it because of his interest in her, or was it something unrelated?

"Yes, but guess what, Chief? You got in my way. I don't think my employer expected you to be there, but it's not my concern what she expected."

"She?" William clung to the word.

St. Joan laughed. "Ah, now, did I say too much?"

"Who?"

"Do you want to hear or not, Chief? This is

my story, not yours, but the point of this dialog is coming, I promise." St. Joan arched a brow. A bird squawked and her eyes darted in the direction of the noise. Her body stayed tense for several moments before she began to move again. "She was a hard one to track in the city. Then I caught the scent in the forest. It's so much easier in the forest. She couldn't hide from me. But you interfered. You saved her from the house. I watched her go in and she did not come back out. She should have burned, so crispy, so pretty and charred." St. Joan rubbed her shoulder. "I don't appreciate being injured."

"My apologies," he mumbled weakly, hoping the sarcasm translated in his slurred voice.

It must have because she opened her mouth and screeched. Birds took off in startled flight. She smiled to herself as she watched them, seeming very pleased with the effect.

She rubbed her shoulder again. "Twice."

He made a confused noise. "Uh…?"

"Twice you bastards injured me," she yelled at him. "You just won't die, at least not by claw, not by fire, not by wreck."

"So you used a tranq gun?"

"Not elegant, I admit, but effective. You see, I decided I don't have to kill you. There are much better ways to inflict damage and make you pay for my injuries." The mountain lion shift swirled in the woman's eyes, fighting to be released. The animal was powerful, perhaps too powerful for the human St. Joan to fight.

"How?" William prompted, trying to keep her from turning. She kept glancing at the sky, as if she might find a meal with the birds she'd stirred up.

"Soon you will need to eat."

"I will be fine," he said.

"You might, but the wolf won't. He'll want to eat, and you'll need to shift to heal. The drugs will keep the human in you from taking control, and in this forest there will only be one thing for you to consume." Her laugh was demented, more so than before. "She will be tasty, Chief, so tasty, and so easy to catch. She's not as strong as you. I smelled her. She neglects her wolf and it is weakened from it. Her hunger will drive her to find you. Yours to find her. When you smell her meat you will not be able to resist it. And when her blood is in your mouth and on your hands, you will never forgive yourself, and the Duncanis will never forgive you. The clans will war, and your peace will be gone into a lifetime of battle and death. Fitting revenge, I think. Such beautiful chaos. My skills come in handy in chaos. So much money to be made."

"You should not have told me this," he said. "I will remember."

"I count on it," she yelled. "Know my name. Know I bested the great Cononious chief. There are many who would thank me for it, many who would offer their protection. Why do you think I took you and not the Duncanis? He is born into his throne. But you? You are just a beggar wolf pretending to be something he's not. All mighty and high. Needs to be knocked down a couple branches off the fake family tree, that is what everyone thinks of you."

Her words stung because there was truth in them. He wasn't born into his station. The old chief chose him. Tobias had been a hard man to know, and a harder adoptive father to love. William was never sure why the chief chose him to be his successor, why he was lifted up so high.

"The bitch will be dead and I will be paid well for it." St. Joan smiled as she made her way to a medicine vial and syringe she'd tossed by the base of a tree. Picking it up, she shoved the dirty needle into the top of the vial and drew out a big dose. "Why don't you nap a bit, Chief, before your big hunt? I need to make arrangement to free your prey."

William tried to kick at her when she got closer to him. She hissed and shoved his leg to the side, twisting him in the air as he hung. Her needle caught his thigh as he swung back, jabbing him hard. He fought the injection but she was quicker. The medicine burned its way into him. Everything became a blur as his limbs deadened into heavy, useless weights.

William opened his mouth, but any threat he would have made was lost under a slacken jaw. His eyes rolled and his head dropped forward. There was nothing he could do.

St. Joan's hand ran onto his cheek as she pulled his face back up to meet hers. He felt her breath on his lips. "She will be so tasty. Happy hunting." As his mind lost the fight with oblivion, he felt warm lips move against his.

TWENTY-ONE

RACHEL DIDN'T MOVE AS THE THIN BALL OF light drew steadily closer, growing in diameter. She stared at it, unsure that it was actually there. After days in darkness, she couldn't trust her eyes. The light bounced, moving up then down in a steady rhythm, like a fat speck of white, glowing cotton caught in the wind. It made its way progressively forward, taking what seemed like hours to cross the inky darkness.

She wasn't sure when it happened, but more specks had appeared behind the first, and their combined glows threw light onto her prison cell. Her eyes ached from endless hours of shifting to see her way in the darkness, a fruitless activity until this moment. She detected a flutter inside the light. Wings? Arms? A tiny smile?

"Fairies?" The small being's body blurred with movement, so it was almost impossible to see more than a glimpse within the shifting motions. Even as her eyes began to recover, it was hard for her shifted vision to focus in on the creatures. When she concentrated her hearing, she could detect a high-pitched buzzing but couldn't make out a language.

Looking beyond the fairies, she saw the inside of her prison for the first time. No wonder she couldn't find a way out. There was no door within the stone hole, only the marks of her claws as she'd tried to dig her way through the walls. The fairies had entered through a crack in the ceiling, near a round hatch. In the dark, the hatch would be undetectable, but now with the light, she could see it carved into the stone.

Her limbs shook as she stood, ignoring the fairies as she reached towards the hatch. She wasn't tall enough. Her arm throbbed where she'd been cut. It had healed over some, but without energy, her body couldn't complete the job. She was so hungry and thirsty from being walled into her prison cell without nourishment, and she knew she wouldn't have lasted much longer. The thought had occurred to her more than once that St. Joan had left her there to die a horrible and slow death.

Rachel rolled a rock under the latch and stood on it. Her legs shook as she fought to keep her balance. The heavy rock lifted a few inches and then fell right back into place. With a grunt, she pushed harder, rising up on her toes. The fairies became agitated, moving faster around her arms and wrists. They helped her without actually touching her. Not one to refuse assistance, she lifted up and pushed harder. The fairies blurred into a thick stream of light. Even her shifter eyes couldn't pick them apart. They pulled harder, lifting her off the ground. Rachel's feet kicked in the air as they hauled her up.

Light streamed in from above as the stone was taken off her hand and tossed aside. A larger being grabbed her fairy-ringed hand and hauled her out of the hole with some difficulty. The woman glowed with an inner light, a shimmering, almost translucent brilliance. The tiny fairies circled up Rachel's arm, moving onto the arm of the light being only to melt into her translucent skin and disappear. As they did so, the woman's features darkened, and the light inside her dimmed until she was flesh.

The woman released her hold, and Rachel fell to her hands and knees on the ground. When she opened her mouth to thank her rescuer, her throat was too tight and dry and she merely croaked.

She'd been right to think of her prison as a grave. Around them, ancient gravestones jutted from the ground.

"You must run, strong one," the woman whispered, her lips barely moving. "Follow me. I will lead you."

Rachel tried to protest, but a light entered the woman's eyes and her body was translucent once more, as fairy lights tore apart her form into a swarm of tiny white dots. They created a trail through the air, drawing her attention to the nearby forest.

Rachel pushed onto her hands and knees and began to crawl. Her naked body, smudged with dirt and blood, and thinned with starvation, had to look strange crawling out from the scarred earth. The graveyard was in an overgrown clearing. Many of the graves had been abandoned by caretakers long ago, left to weather and age beneath a dense overgrowth of weeds. One grave stood out because of the care it had been recently given. A strange skull was carved into the top with wings sprouting from the side of its head. Beneath the carving, the grave marker read, "Here lyes buried the body of Mr. Samuel St. Joan who departed this life August ye 16th 1901 in ye 162nd year of his age."

Rachel didn't think too hard on it as she

crawled past. The fairy lights were pulling further away, and she'd lose track of them soon if she didn't hurry. Shifting always hurt, but this time was worse. She cried out as she dragged herself forward. Joints popped and muscles stretched so hard they tore. Her human cries turned to the whimper of an injured wolf as she limped along the graves towards the forest.

Each step burned. She willed the fairy lights to slow down and circle back. She heard the buzzing noise they made, but it was too hard to concentrate on sounds that far away. By sheer willpower and determination she managed to limp her way into the forest. The calming scent of wild nature rolled over her like aromatherapy. She breathed deeply, taking in her surroundings, letting them become a part of her.

The ache in her stomach worsened as the pain in her limbs subsided. She resisted the urge to hunt in the forest, though the primal drive was strong. As a wolf, raw meat satiated on a base level, but with a human consciousness, she couldn't bring herself to hunt prey for food. A tremor worked over her and she jerked, partially shifting back into human form. She cried out, a half scream, half whine.

Rachel tried to hold the shift so she could heal faster, but it was too hard. Her body jerked again, and she rolled onto her back to finish her transformation. When fur became flesh, she stayed on the ground, breathing hard. The fairy lights were gone, not that she could see too far because of the trees. Not knowing what else to do, she rolled over and pushed herself to her feet. Naked, dirty and sore, she put one foot in front of the other and stumbled her way down the narrowly beaten path. The woods didn't scare her. She could handle the woods. It was the being lost and naked in a foreign country part that bothered her.

Limping along, she held her waist, trying to ignore her growling stomach and aching head. Not that she wasn't grateful for the help, but she really wished her rescuer wouldn't have taken off so fast.

"Beggars can't be choosers," she whispered, renewing her determination.

TWENTY-TWO

"We always liked you, Duncanis."

Douglas eyed the tiny fairies as they swarmed around his panther head. They were a sub-species of fairy, brought forth centuries ago with an ancient magic long since abandoned. The tiny creatures were of one mind and many bodies. It was said a spell blasted a single fairy into many parts.

Those parts began melting together in front of him until a single, solid woman kneeled on the ground. When they were one, Rara continued, "I always thought you a powerful creature. I like cats."

Rara reached out to pet him. Her skin shimmered when she touched him. There was power in her, so much power, and yet she would not use it for much beyond an enticement for pleasure. Fairies could not help themselves. They were all things natural and reproductive. They were fertility to the earth, new life and old death. Their bodies were made of the seasons.

Douglas lifted his head and closed his eyes as he shifted to human form. He stayed on his hands and knees. "Have you seen the Cononious chief?"

"Is that why you summoned me here to the sacred stone?" Rara looked to the nearby offering table to the pile of leaves and flowers he'd thrown on top.

"Yes. I am looking for the chief, and a woman who may be with him. She's special. I must find them."

"Special?" Rara shook her head. "St. Joan is many things, but not special. Those shifted lips I have tasted in return of a favor. She is strong and replenished me. She tastes of the forest, and of the river, but there is nothing special in that."

"So you have seen her? With the chief? What about Rachel? Was there another woman with them?" Douglas pushed back on his heels. "Please, you must tell me."

"I must do nothing without the price being paid." Rara gave him a meaningful look. Her eyes moved down to his cock.

"I would," Douglas lied, "but to do so would mean your death."

Why did every fairy insist on trying to seduce his kind? Yes, shifters had a potent sexual energy that fairies had a strange fascination with, but it was to the point they all had a death wish. Fairies made that energy worse with the very pheromones they released when aroused. It fell onto the shifter to be strong, for the two races did not blend together well. Every century a shifter would try it, thinking they could control it, and every century his kind would be reminded of reality by the bloody mess that resulted from the joining.

Rara pouted. "Shifters." She turned to leave him. Her body became translucent as part of her left arm flew away.

"But I can ensure you get an audience with Kristoff." Douglas reached for her right arm to keep her from leaving.

"Mm, vampires." She smiled. Vampires were notoriously hard to find for fairies. They ran in much different circles. Vampires preferred to live next to big cities where the food supplies were. Fairies avoided humans. Both tended to be flighty and did not stay long in one place.

"Vampire king," Douglas corrected.

"A little blood and he will last a week." Rara

nodded. The fairies from her arm hovered over them. "It is agreed. Ask us."

"Was another woman with St. Joan and the chief? Her name is Rachel."

Rara shook her head. "No. She was not with them."

Douglas felt disappointment slam into his chest. His heart pounded wildly. He didn't like the fear that washed over him. He began to shake. Weakly, he said, "I need you to lead me to the Cononious chief."

She nodded. "Try to keep up. The last wolf did not follow so well."

"Wait, what wolf?" Douglas demanded. He'd started to let go of her arm only to tighten his grip. She yelped and her arm exploded into tiny fairy lights. They danced around the forest away from his reach as Rara stood, armless, before him.

"The woman shifter St. Joan kissed me to free for her. Poor wolf was trapped underground. I would have said no, but St. Joan is a shifter, and she seemed busy with the Cononious chief playing in the forest. I tried to get the wolf to follow me, but you summoned me here and the wolf did not keep up." Rara smiled. Some of the fairy lights came forward to move along his naked spine. His flesh tingled with pleasure, but he resisted the drugging euphoria of her touch. His body did not want the fairy woman. He wanted Rachel. Only Rachel.

"That is the woman I seek. St. Joan did not want to rescue her. She wants to kill her. You must tell me where—"

"Kill?" Rara narrowed her eyes. Her body jerked back from him as if blasted by a hurricane. She burst into lights, swirling angrily in the air. Her voice became a buzzing chorus of sounds that he could barely understand. He spoke many languages, but rarely had a need to listen to fairies gossiping in their native tongue. "I will have no part of killing, Duncanis!"

Like an enraged swarm of bees, the fairies dashed into the forest. Douglas shifted, surging after them. He supposed saving William should have played more heavily in his mind, but the Cononious chief knew the risk of their stations. Rachel did not. This was the closest he'd been to finding Rachel since she disappeared. He couldn't lose her trail now. Besides, William would want him to rescue their future wife first.

TWENTY-THREE

WILLIAM WOKE UP ALREADY SHIFTED, BLEEDING, hungry and very confused. He growled frantically as he sniffed the air. Meat. He needed meat. His jaw snapped as he watched birds fly overhead. Jumping, he tried to catch them at their impossible height. Then another scent lingered over him, just beyond a strange concentration of fairy urine marking the forest floor.

Meat. His primal mind whispered to him as he growled and surged into the forest. The one thought lingered desperately in his mind, drumming in rhythm from his brain to his running feet. *Meat. Meat. Meat…*

His vision tunneled as he sped through the forest. The stretch of his muscles felt good against his many wounds. The scent of live prey became stronger. The beast inside him had complete control. A flash of pink flesh showed in the trees, standing out against the brown and green. He darted right, then left, dodging fallen logs as he left the path. His prey turned as he burst forward through the brush. He didn't think, didn't stop. His teeth found tender, soft flesh. Blood filled his mouth and he clamped down harder. A scream pierced the air, but the sound only fueled his feverish predatory drive.

Meat.

           ❧

DOUGLAS KEPT THE SCENT OF THE FAIRIES IN HIS nose as he chased them through the forest. Miles melted beneath his paws. He didn't care if he had to run to the end of the earth to find Rachel. He would save her.

Desperation filled him. If he lost her he wasn't sure what he would do. When he caught up to Rara, she was standing in solid form before a tree. She pointed at it. Douglas sniffed the blood-soaked air. William's scent was strong. Ropes had been cut and discarded on the ground. Nearby, the charred earth attested to a fire pit.

"This place smells like a fairy's toilet," Rara

said in displeasure. "Such things are not done in the forest. St. Joan tries to hide herself from you."

Rara burst into the smaller, dancing lights and filtered back into the trees, this time much slower than before. Douglas did not wonder at the fairy's changing moods, from anger to irritation to indifference, for fairies had notoriously short attention spans.

Douglas moved away from the bloody tree and began to circle the abandoned campsite. Ringing around the area twice, he caught the faintest hint of William's scent and began to slowly track it through the woods.

❧

RACHEL SCREAMED AS THE WOLF TIGHTENED ITS hold on her arm. It took her a moment to recognize William in her surprise. He was so strong and her body weak from starvation. She'd resisted the urge to hunt too long. When her distaste for killing was finally outdone by her need for food, it had been too late. She had been too weak to run the woods.

She'd been stumbling aimlessly in her human form, searching for berries or water, when William found her. His teeth pressed deeper. She hit him on the side of the head with her fist as they twisted on the ground. Dirt flew around them, a thick and choking cloud. Her fist flew back, striking a stone. Without thought, she grabbed it and hit him again. He yelped and let go. Blood trickled down her flesh, the gush made worse by the hard pumping of her heart. She rolled from him with the sheer force of adrenaline and threw the rock at his head. It struck him in the nose.

"William," she yelled. His grey body she would know anywhere, but something was off about his eyes. "William, stop. It's me. It's Rachel."

She breathed hard. The blood loss started to make her dizzy. She lifted her arm, trying to hold it above her head. Blood trailed down her side and the limb dropped weakly.

"William," she whispered as he circled her. He growled low in this throat. "Please. Rachel. I'm Rachel."

Rachel fell to her knees, unable to control the shifting of her body as it went into defensive mode. She knew if the wolf overtook her, she'd fight to the death—her death.

Survival kicked in. Her body strained with the shift. Feathers sprouted from her arms as she fought the wolf inside her, only to smooth over with the flexible collagenous fibers of her shark skin. It had been a long time since that form tried to overtake her. The shifting war inside her body burned. She screamed in pain.

"Rachel," a hoarse voice said. She caught a glimpse of William shifting back. The wild hunger had left his eyes as he crawled near her. His naked body was smeared with mud and blood. "Bloody hell, what did I do?"

Shaking hands touched her and the shifting war instantly calmed. Her body jerked as she looked up at him. He cradled her arm where he'd bitten her, examining it with a look of horror and pain.

"What did I do? What did I do?" he repeated over and over again.

Rachel wanted to reassure him, to swipe the agony from his eyes, even as the current white heat of pain radiating over her arm was his doing. She twitched on the ground. He leaned in and tried to kiss her, but hesitated and pulled back.

"You're not healing. We have to heal you," he said. "What did I do?"

🐾

WILLIAM TRIED NOT TO MOVE RACHEL ON THE ground as he looked around the forest for help. There was none, only Rachel bleeding from where he'd nearly torn her arm from her body.

The gash was horrible to look at, the limb raw and limp.

The only way he knew was to give her his energy through sex, but how could he make love to her after what he'd done. He saw the pain in her eyes, was pretty sure there was anger there too. How could he kiss her? Make love to her? Like this? After that?

"Rachel, I'm sorry. I don't know how else to help you." In truth, after what he'd been through, after the cutting and the drugs at St. Joan's hands, he didn't feel stable enough to help her. He felt the pull of the wolf inside him. If he gave her his energy, would he simply turn wild again and attack to regain it back? "I would give you everything I am to save you."

"Kill her!"

William jerked, instantly taking a protective stance over Rachel's body.

"I said kill her now! Why did you stop? You shouldn't have stopped." St. Joan stood a few feet away. The overbearingly strong scent of fairy urine radiated from her, masking her scent completely. He ignored the odor as he faced her. She stepped to the side to get a better view of Rachel. Her feral eyes shone with victory. "Mm, that is a nasty cut. No worries, Chief, she'll die soon. Very soon." Her mouth parted and she made a biting gesture into the air. "Just in time for the Duncanis to say goodbye and see what you have done."

William didn't think. He charged forth. St. Joan squeaked and leapt backward, as if surprised at the attack.

Desperate and hungry, William didn't think. He shifted in the air seconds before taking the treacherous woman by her throat. St. Joan shifted beneath his teeth and he bit harder. Scratching fingernails turned to claws as she fought him. Her blood assuaged the beast in him as he tore flesh. The mindless hunger would be appeased.

TWENTY-FOUR

"WILLIAM! WHAT HAS HAPPENED HERE?" Douglas took in the bloody battlefield of the clearing. Around them the forest was quiet, as if the fray had scared away all living creatures.

When William transformed, he was sitting on the ground next to the corpse of the mountain lion. "Rachel. Heal Rachel."

Douglas was already on his way to her side. She moaned softly when he touched her. "What the hell happened here?"

Her face was barely recognizable beneath the wild, tangled hair and dirty skin. He didn't care. Relief rose up in him. He had found her. Only the emotion didn't last long as he realized she wasn't moving. Without thinking, he kissed her, willing her to respond, to take whatever she needed from his body.

"My forest is not a toilet, St. Joan!" came Rara's voice.

He opened his eyes but didn't stop kissing Rachel. Her lips became warmer against his, but still didn't respond as they should have. Rara kicked the dead mountain lion on the ground, ignoring William. The Cononious chief did not move from his place as he stared at Rachel.

"And I did not save her to kill her," Rara continued, kicking the body again. "This is my forest."

Douglas pulled back, unable to get Rachel to answer him. "Rara, please, can you undo what was done."

Rara stopped mid-kick and moved to Douglas and Rachel. She stood over them. "I did not save her to kill her, so I will save her again."

The fairy leaned over and touched Douglas's upturned face. "But first, you must kiss me."

"There is no time. We—" Douglas protested, only to stop.

"Agree to pay my price," Rara demanded. He nodded in agreement. She looked at William and demanded the same. William gave a weak nod, not seeming to really hear her. The Cononious chief didn't move.

"Mm," Rara moaned as she went to her knees. She wrapped her arms around Douglas and pressed an open-mouthed kiss to him. He felt her tongue slide into his mouth, probing. Everywhere she touched, he tingled. His heart began to beat hard. Fairy pheromones were impossible to resist. His cock thickened.

Rara pulled away first. Douglas tried to follow her with his mouth. She gave him one last peck and then turned her attention to the woman on the ground. Douglas watched as Rara moved to kiss Rachel's still mouth as she had him. That's when he realized his hand was on Rachel's breast, massaging it. Rachel moaned and moved beneath his hand. Her naked legs stirred against him.

Rara pulled away, breathing hard. Her body shimmered with translucent blue. "Mm, shifters. So much power."

When Rachel looked up at him, her eyes swam with the same translucent blue light Rara illuminated. It mixed with the shifter's silver. Unable to resist the woman he loved, Douglas kissed her. This time she responded. One hand lifted to his face, holding him to her kiss. Her lips parted wide to let him devour her. The injured limb did not move from the ground.

They were already naked from running wildly about the forest. When her legs opened wider, he didn't need more of an invite. He drew his hips along her thighs and thrust into her. His cock slid into her wet sex, slamming hard. Fuck, but it felt nice. All the fear and desperation of the last several days poured out of him into her. With each thrust, her body became stronger in its responses. Her injured limb bumped along his arm briefly before falling to the ground.

Douglas lifted up. The grit of dirt slid between them. He didn't care. Rachel met his thrusts with her own. She bucked off the ground. Her eyes fairly glowed with the fairy's transferred power. Douglas felt Rara's fingers glide down his spine. The tingling sensation was too much. He jerked his release into her, giving Rachel all the energy he could spare. She cried out softly.

As soon as he'd finished, Rachel pushed on his arm with a low growl. He rolled onto his back, completely drained and unable to move.

❧

WILLIAM WATCHED DOUGLAS HEAL RACHEL, torn between the normal jealousies he felt each time the other two were together and the desire for the Duncanis chief to save the woman they loved. The fairy, Rara, tried to kiss him too, but he'd jerked his head away from her. Not to be denied her fun, the fairy exploded into her tiny counterparts and began swarming his chest, back, hips and legs. They concentrated on his cock and the tingling caused the shaft to lift. He stared intently at Rachel and Douglas, as the fairy lights stroked him.

William tried to swat them away, but they merely scattered and returned in full force. They centered their efforts on his cock and balls. Their touches were as light as air and as potent as one of the best blow jobs he'd ever gotten. He tried to resist. His fingers dug into the dirt of the forest floor. Unbidden, his hips lifted off the ground. His body mimicked the motion of Douglas's thrusts. Then, as the Duncanis chief found his release, so too did William. The fairy lights left his body, having gotten what they wanted off him. Had circumstances been different, had he been stronger, their attentions would have caused him to ravish Rara until there was nothing left.

Rachel shoved the Duncanis chief off her body and instantly crawled towards William on her hands and knees. Her injured arm gave out a little bit when she put weight on it, but that did not hamper her progress. Her glowing, blue eyes pierced him.

Behind Rachel, Douglas didn't move. The fairy lights went to his drained body and took advantage, just as they had with the Cononious chief. Rara formed into full body and straddled the man's waist. Douglas tried to push her off, but Rara said, "Fight if you will, but it is not rape. You agreed to pay my price in return for saving the shifter woman, and I aim to collect what is due, Duncanis."

Douglas was too weak as the fairy stroked his cock to full length and began to ride him like the airy, free spirit she was.

William drew his eyes back to Rachel as she instantly grabbed his spent cock. With a few strokes, she had it lifted to full capacity. He tried to touch her cheek gently, looking past the euphoric fire in her eyes. "Rachel, I'm sorry. I didn't want to hurt you. I'll never forgive myself for—"

Rachel cut off his words with a passionate kiss. She pushed him onto his back, rolling down with him. When she lifted up, she reached between their bodies to stroke his cock before moving it to her pussy. The glide of her body on his was too much. No part of him wanted to protest. Anything she wanted from him, she would have. He had not been strong enough to save her earlier, so now he would let her drain every last bit of life he had left if she so wanted it.

For a long moment, the sounds of a dirty orgy filled the forest. The women rode the men beneath them like wild creatures. William grabbed hold of Rachel's breasts, only to glide his fingers down to her hips to help drive her onto his cock. Douglas tried to fight Rara, but his energy-drained body was no match for her fairy pheromones.

William's ass slid on the ground. Twigs and stones from the forest floor bit into his flesh. He let the wild woman on his cock do what she wanted. Fuck, but she was beautiful! It was all he could to do to hold back his release as he waited for her to find her climax. Suddenly, Rachel tensed. Her sex clamped down on him hard. It was all the invitation he needed. He came inside her, filling her with his seed and with his very life force. The wounds on her injured arm healed completely. Her glowing eyes began to dim. She didn't move off his cock, as she sat on his waist.

"Do summon me again should you need a favor," Rara said from atop Douglas. "And do not think I have forgotten the audience you promised to give me with the vampire king. Do not make me wait long, or I will come to our court and ensorcel all shifters within my reach."

The fairy burst into bright lights and floated away on the breeze. Douglas rolled onto his hands and knees and crawled towards the others. Rachel finally pulled off William's cock and moved to sit beside him. She rubbed her arm. For a moment, no one spoke.

TWENTY-FIVE

"What happened?" Rachel asked, confused. Her words broke the silence as she turned her eyes to where the fairy lights were disappearing overhead. She gave an accusing look at Douglas. Had she just imagined what she saw? Much of their current situation was a blur, but she was pretty sure she just saw Douglas fucking another woman. "You—"

She stopped herself. What right did she have to demand he not fuck anyone but her? She'd just been riding William a few feet away. Yet, somehow, her riding William was different. William had been a part of their arrangement from the very beginning.

"It's not what you think," Douglas said.

"He did not have a choice," William added. "He had to."

Rachel stepped away from both of them. She glanced at Douglas's cock and frowned.

"*We* had to," Douglas corrected in irritation. He shot William a hard look. "It was the only way to get her to agree to help us save you."

"It changes nothing," William said.

She rubbed her arm again. The deep ache would not go away. It was strange considering she'd just had sex—twice, if she was remembering correctly. First Douglas fucked her, then she fucked William. And apparently, they both fucked a fairy whore. Douglas tried to reach for her but she jerked from him, again glancing at his cock. She imagined she could still see the fairy's pleasure moistening it. The thought stung. On one hand it was erotic as hell, on another it caused a fierce, possessive jealousy to well up inside her. And William. He was just as bad. She looked down at him on the ground. His cock had touched the fairy as well.

"We should have claimed her, then Rara wouldn't have been able to seduce us," William said.

"You should have kept your jaws shut, wolf," Douglas growled.

William couldn't meet her gaze. She rubbed

her arm again, and asked, "You did this to me, William?"

"St. Joan drugged me. I did not mean…I did not…" William looked behind him to where the dead, mountain lion body of St. Joan had fallen. "I have no excuse for what happened. I would give my life never to have harmed you. I love you, Rachel. I could never willingly harm you."

"*We* love you, Rachel," Douglas asserted. "We should have married you the second we found you."

"You mean the second you found out I was an omni-shifter." Rachel wrapped her arms around her naked chest. She became aware of their surroundings, of her dirty flesh, of the dead cat on the ground. The men were no better off with their filthy, bloodstained bodies. Before they could protest, she said, "I don't feel so well. I haven't eaten. My arm hurts and my head is throbbing. Can we just get out of here?"

"Yes," William said, standing. "Anything you desire."

"Of course," Douglas said. "Can you run? Or shall we carry you?"

As much as the idea of running sounded like a horrible plan, she didn't want them touching her until she had time to think clearly. "I can walk."

TWENTY-SIX

Rachel was sure she'd never been so happy to see a bed in her life. She fell into it and intended to never move. After the threesome appeared through the servant's entrance of William's home, naked and covered in forest litter, the entire estate had become abuzz with activity. She felt it around them, pouring through the walls with gossipy excitement.

Magda had been less than pleased to see them. Her pursed lips and pruned expression only worsened with each passing second. She'd quickly ushered them into separate rooms to bathe and change. In fact, before slamming the door behind Rachel, the woman had ordered her to bathe the wild off and to not leave the room as food would be brought to her.

Rachel hardly cared. Shower, food, bed, that's all she wanted at the moment. The rest of it could wait until later.

❖

WILLIAM LOOKED AT MAGDA AS SHE STOOD IN the center of his bedroom. Her hands were placed disapprovingly on her hips. He knew she had been worried about him, even if she would never show it. The old woman wanted every detail of his kidnapping, details he refused to give.

"I told you, I was drugged most of the time. It doesn't matter now anyway. St. Joan is no longer a threat." William tossed his towel aside and opened the wardrobe where he kept his sweatpants. He pulled them on, not caring that Magda saw him naked. "We are all safely returned. That is all that matters."

He didn't believe his own words. What happened did matter. Drugged or not, he'd almost killed Rachel. Fear gripped him. He wouldn't have been able to live with the guilt, or the loss. The fact only cemented what he had known since first seeing her—he loved her, he wanted her, and she would be his chieftess.

"But St. Joan? Did she say who hired her?" Magda insisted.

"Only that it was a woman," William answered absently, as he reached for a T-shirt. Instead of grabbing it, he let his hand drop.

"Do you suspect anyone?"

He slowly closed the wardrobe. "Should I?"

"No," she answered, a little too quickly. He turned to look at her, studying her emotionless face. "I suppose it could be one of the old families. Plenty of women wish to be your bride. You have turned down meeting many of the eligible women from some very powerful families. I warned you that they might feel slighted."

"Or perhaps it is someone here at court," he said. "Someone close."

"Who do you think?" Magda pondered. "Ginger? She always seemed a bit reckless and wild to me."

"Then why do you continually try to get me to marry her?" William crossed his arms over his chest. He was tired and not in the mood to discuss anything. Yet duty forced him to remain on his feet and to listen.

"Her father is influential and wildness can be tamed with persistence," Magda said.

"Then why do you oppose Rachel? You said she was wild."

"Feral more like it," Magda mumbled before quickly amending, "Wildness can be tamed with persistence so long as the proper breeding and background is there to support it. Rachel is an American. They have a different kind of wildness to them. She was raised in the woods. If you would have read my report I gave you when you landed, you would have seen the kind of shifters she comes from. Elvie Dunne had a reputation for bedding down with several men. She never mated to one. That is who raised Rachel. It is hard enough sharing a bride and getting our natural instincts to accept a three-way mate, but there is always a risk if the bride is promiscuous by nature."

"Promiscuous? Rachel is not Elvie." Anger boiled inside him that Magda would dare to say such a thing.

He thought of the first time he'd met Rachel. Within seconds she'd been in his arms and on his cock. He pushed the thought aside. It meant nothing beyond that their desire for each other was natural. Plus, she'd been so tight on him. He would have known if she'd had sex recently, especially promiscuous sex with numerous partners, right?

"And she is also not a lady. This is our chance to put an English rose on the shifter throne, a Cononious bride. Rachel is Duncanis. We need a Cononious bride, William. Why not choose

Lisbetha? She is willing. She is pretty. She is meek. Her shift is rare. And she is one of us in all things, by birthright, by clan, by ancestry."

"And she does nothing to my blood," William growled. "She would be a pretty ornament I would quickly grow tired of looking at."

"What does a chief's marriage have to do with boiling blood? You have a duty to your people, a duty beyond petty sex. If you must know the truth of it, if you grow weary of Lisbetha, then you can take a lover. Chiefs have done it in the past. Great lengths must be taken to keep the affairs quiet for the sake of peace, but it has been done. There are protocols in place. I had hoped it would not be necessary to have this conversation with you so soon, but there it is."

Her words did little to comfort him. The idea of a loveless life tore at his soul. Well, loveless wasn't exactly true. He would have the love of his people, and his love for them. Would that be enough?

"We have decided, Magda. We want Rachel." William had never been so sure of anything in his life. "Perhaps the American blood will do the old clans some good and bring the American shifters back to us."

Her face tightened in shock. She gave a small shake of her head, as if the gesture could take back the certainty of his words. Finally, she managed, "You have had a long ordeal. I will leave you to rest and we will discuss this at a later time. Nothing has to be announced tonight. Now that you are back I will reschedule the ball. Lisbetha has been a great help in the planning." She gave a small nod. "My chief."

As Magda left the room, William moved to sit on the edge of his bed. His bare feet dug into the thick carpet and he curled his toes against it. Perhaps sleep was the best thing for him at the moment.

❖

"SHE DID NOT SPEAK THE ENTIRE WAY HOME," William said, his voice weary.

"I know, I was there," Douglas answered. He'd come to William's room after his shower just as Magda was leaving it. William wore a pair of sweatpants and Douglas a pair of pajama pants. It was rare they allowed themselves to sit so comfortably attired in the presence of another person, aside from the nakedness caused by shifting. However, this situation was anything but comfortable.

Douglas couldn't help the anger he felt towards

William. The man had almost killed Rachel in the attack. Irrational as it was, he kept thinking that the man should have been stronger, should have found a way to stop St. Joan, to fight the drugs she'd given him and the very nature of the wolf inside him. Had he been in the same position, Douglas was not so sure events would have happened differently, though. It didn't stop his anger, much of which was born out of the fear of losing Rachel.

"I told Magda that we intend to marry Rachel. I assume that is still your wish?" William rubbed his tired eyes.

"Of course it is my wish. Had we claimed her as ours immediately, then we would not have been in a position for Rara to do what she did." Douglas pulled in a hard breath and held it. His hands worked in agitation as he paced the room.

"Do you think she will forgive us for it? There is no hiding it from her." William rolled his neck back and forth, staring at the ceiling.

"I will explain it to her. I will simply tell her the way of things. If we did not get Rara to agree to help us by using her pheromones, Rachel wouldn't have responded to our touch and she would have died. We did it to save her. It is the truth. Rachel is a smart woman. She will listen to reason."

William raised a doubtful brow but did not protest the plan.

"It is decided then? We make her our bride as soon as etiquette allows." Douglas's words were more of a decree than a question.

William nodded in agreement. "The ball is being re-planned as we speak. I see no reason it cannot be done then."

"Agreed." Douglas nodded and moved quickly from the room. He strode purposefully down the hall, stopping to look at Rachel's door. He wanted to go in, wanted to touch her, to be with her tonight.

"You should let her rest," William said from down the hall. "We agreed."

Douglas nodded and stormed away from the Cononious chief. "Just don't forget that it is my turn to be with her."

TWENTY-SEVEN

"DID YOU HONESTLY JUST SAY YOU TWO HAD SEX with another woman for me?" Rachel glared at the two men standing in front of her in her guest bedroom. Like all the other rooms in the manor, it was decadent and perfect, like some twelve-star hotel only royalty and celebrities could get into. Douglas had looked so earnest as he tried to explain it, and William would not meet her eyes. In fact, William had little to say beyond observing that she looked rested. "In what universe is that even a viable defense?" She dropped her voice in a poor imitation of a male speaker, "I slept with that woman for you, baby."

William and Douglas shared a look.

"Omigod, you're right," she said. "I have no

room to speak. I sleep with both of you and you don't complain about it."

"We did not say anything," William said. She ignored him. She'd seen the knowing look they had given each other.

"I'm acting like some kind of shrewish girlfriend. Of course this is an open relationship." She hated the words but knew they were the logical, adult, reasonable thing to say.

Damn reasonable adult logic anyway!

"This is not an open relationship," Douglas stated firmly. He lifted a finger towards her to punctuate his point. He wore a white dress shirt and black slacks. His black leather belt sported a bright silver buckle that automatically drew the eyes down to his waist. She didn't need the reminder of how potent a lover he was. That fact was never far from her mind. His dark hair framed his even darker eyes.

William was a contrast next to him, blond-haired and blue-eyed. His dark blue shirt brought out his eyes in such a way as to make them mesmerizing all on their own. His gray slacks hugged his hips and ass, only to loosen around his legs. Her eyes went back up, trying to catch his. Those eyes made her tremble all the way to her toes. A woman could easily melt in his gaze.

Individually, these men were powerful and

desirable in their own right. Together, they were a potent force. How could any woman resist them?

"What kind of craziness have you brought me into?" Rachel whispered, more to herself than to them. "This is crazy. I don't know why we're even discussing this. You're royalty, both of you. I'm just some girl from America who apparently is supposed to be running a wilderness sanctuary. We come from literally different worlds. Now St. Joan is gone, the threat is over. I can go home."

"The threat is not over. The person who hired St. Joan is still out there," William interrupted. He had been avoiding her eyes and now finally looked at her. "When I was held prisoner I learned only that a female hired her to kill you. We weren't expected to be at the sanctuary and were merely obstacles to her real target—you. She was angered that we interrupted her little fire show and came after us as personal revenge. With her gone, we are safe, but…" William gave Douglas a concerned look.

"It is not safe for you to leave us," Douglas said bluntly. "We will keep you safe. I've already ordered Duncanis guards to keep watch."

"The Cononious guards have this place well in hand," William protested.

"Obviously not, considering what happened," Douglas countered.

The men continued to argue. Rachel watched in stunned silence. She'd never seen them like this, not towards each other. She lifted her hand to interrupt, but couldn't get a word in.

"Your guards let her run the forest alone," Douglas yelled.

"She is not a prisoner. I saw no reason to order them to stop her. How was I to know she'd just run off like that," William returned.

"Ah, hey—" Rachel tried to insert.

"There is a killer on the loose. Of course she should be stopped!" Douglas took an aggressive step forward, his eyes filling with silver.

"*Was* on the loose. St. Joan is dead thanks to me." William met his challenge, puffing out his chest.

"Rachel almost died *thanks to you*." Douglas poked William in the shoulder.

"Guys, seriously—" Rachel tried again. They ignored her.

"And your solution was to get Rara?" William gave a derisive laugh before pushing back. "We'll be lucky if Rachel will let us touch her again after that."

Douglas stumbled but caught his footing. "Do not blame me, at least I did something!"

"I almost prefer you shifted. As a man you are rash and bossy," William grumbled.

"And I prefer you shifted. As a man you are mild and indecisive. Tobias gave you his throne and you walk around as if it is some burden, something to be scared of. No wonder St. Joan came after you. As a Cononious she would hardly be worried about taking out a weak leader. Find your balls, William, and use them already. Take your throne. Take your clan. Answer to no one but me."

"Seriously—" Rachel said, raising her voice to be heard over their fighting.

William's answer was to punch Douglas across the jaw. Douglas responded with a punch of his own. Soon the men were wrestling each other to the ground, swinging fists and knees into their opponent. Rachel watched in horror, demanding they stop at once. They didn't hear her, or if they did, they didn't listen.

Material ripped and buttons flew in her direction. She dodged one before moving forward to try to physically stop them. When she grabbed hold of William's arm, Douglas used the opening to throw another punch. When she pulled at Douglas's hair, William kicked the man in the side of the thigh, causing the Duncanis chief to fall onto his side on the floor.

Rachel brushed strands of Douglas's dark hair from her fingers. "Fine. You two might as well keep fucking going at each other because I've fucking had it with the both of you!"

Instantly both froze and turned to her. William had Douglas pinned on the ground. Douglas's hand gripped William's torn shirt. Rachel gasped, surprised at the quick ending to their argument.

"Did you say…?" William began.

"Fuck?" Douglas finished.

"You are such guys. Out of everything that just happened, the only thing you comprehend is the word fuck." She rolled her eyes at them and shook her head in irritation. "Unbelievable."

"We were just blowing off steam," Douglas said, by way of excuse. "Don't be mad, lass."

"Had to be said and now it is," William added. "Everything is fine, sweetheart. Now about this fucking…"

Douglas let go of William's shirt. William rolled back, letting Douglas off the ground. A dark bruise ringed an even darker eye on Douglas, while William's cheek had a tiny cut on it.

"We could use some healing." Douglas rubbed his elbow and winced. She didn't buy his injured act for a minute.

Rachel saw their flushed cheeks and bright, silver-threaded eyes. Their blood was pumping hard in their veins. The brawl would only have heightened their primal instincts.

"No one would have to know," William said. "Just like on the plane."

"Our secret," Douglas agreed.

Rachel took a step back, realizing their intent was a joint seduction. "Oh no you don't. I'm still mad at you."

The back of her legs hit the foot of the bed. They crowded forward, blocking every retreat but the one that would take her onto the mattress.

Douglas touched her arm. "Let us make it up to you."

"Come on, Rachel, let us have a little celebration of the upcoming…"

"Celebration of…?" she asked, suddenly nervous.

"Of life," William quickly said. She wondered what he had actually meant and had the distinct feeling he wasn't telling her something. "Celebration of life."

"It's my turn to go first," Douglas said, pushing his hips forward so his cock brushed alongside her hip.

"So long as you don't wear her out for my turn," William said.

"You jackasses realize I can hear you, right?" Rachel pushed at both of their chests. They didn't move. William brought his hips forward and moaned softly. "Are you both telling me you're really keeping track as to whose turn it is?"

"Of course," they answered in unison.

"Out of fairness," Douglas said.

"Unless you decree otherwise," William added.

"Or the other one is not available and you have needs."

"Or if you are fighting with one of us and have needs the other can fulfill but you don't want them to because you're angry."

"Or—"

"I think I got it." Rachel couldn't help it as she chuckled. "But I also think it's a little unromantic of you two to be counting how many times we have sex."

"Not how many times, just whose turn it is," Douglas clarified. "And it's my turn."

Rachel arched a brow before ordering Douglas, "Take off your clothes and go lie on the bed."

Douglas tore at his shirt, ripping out of it as he crawled onto the mattress to do as she commanded. He fumbled with his pants to get them off before tossing them across the room. Within seconds, he was naked and on his back. William took a deep breath and stepped back to let her go.

"So long as we're clear that I'm still mad at both of you. And this conversation is far from over." She gave them a pointed look.

William nodded. "Of course."

"If you say so," Douglas said.

"You too," she ordered William, "out of your clothes."

William gave her a playful smile as he obeyed. Rachel was slower to undress, pulling out of the cotton shirt and slacks Magda had left for her in the room. Then, turning to Douglas, she crawled over him.

"I'm not some ride you take turns on," Rachel said. On her hands and knees over Douglas, she put her ass towards William. Douglas's cock towered beneath her. She moved her mouth to kiss the tip. He jerked and the tip leaked pre-cum. "I'm not a toy to be shared between the two of you. If I hear you talking about whose turn it is ever again, it will be no one's turn. Understand?"

The men didn't answer. Douglas was too busy reaching for her breasts. William moaned and began rubbing her hips from behind. She wiggled her ass towards William. He took the invitation eagerly, kneeling behind her on the bed.

"But, it's my…" Douglas looked as if he might protest. "You are really beautiful, lass."

"That's what I thought." She gave Douglas a

half smile before leaning over to suck his cock gently into her mouth, shutting him up. His hands wound into her hair, keeping her mouth on him as he groaned in approval.

William's cock brushed her wet sex, moving along the lips. His hands ran along her back and hips, before coming around to hold her breasts. She moaned against the dick in her mouth.

Douglas held her tight against him. His muscles flexed beneath her. She placed her hands next to his hips, supporting her weight. William entered her slowly from behind, taking his time as he slid halfway in before withdrawing. Soon her mouth mimicked William's movements.

A spell wove its way around them. Not the mindless euphoria of the fairies, but something much older and much more real. She felt her body pull in two directions. She wanted both of them, needed both of them. The depth of the emotion scared her. By all rights, she should have been angry with them. Well, if not *by all rights*, then by some sort of feminine entitlement logic. The wave of possessiveness surprised her. She wanted to bite them, claim them somehow so no other woman would dare look at her territory.

Her movements became more aggressive. The need inside them was too strong to fight. Douglas tensed against her mouth, spilling his seed between her lips. Behind her, William kept moving, deeper and faster. She gasped for air, bringing her head sharply back. Her body tensed, jerking suddenly as she was racked with pleasure. Seconds later, William's soft, climactic cry washed over her.

William let go of her hips and she fell forward to lie against Douglas's chest. She slid against him to stretch out along his side. William crawled next to her, sandwiching her between the two men.

There was a strange, serene pleasure to the moment. None of them spoke. Rachel closed her eyes, feeling their calm presence next to her on the bed. The back of Douglas's hand brushed against hers and their fingers twined. She ran her hand onto William's thigh and let it rest.

Rachel wasn't sure how much time passed as she dozed next to them. Douglas moved, turning towards her, stirring her from her sleep. Her head rolled onto his arm as her hand slid up from William's thigh to his chest.

"You never asked me why I ran after you ordered me not to leave the manor," she said, completely relaxed.

"Why?" both men asked in unison, their voices sleepy.

"I heard you talking." Rachel turned her head towards William and drew her hand up to touch

Douglas's chest as well. "I know you think to make me your chieftess queen, and that you had no intention of telling me about your marriage plans for us."

Both men stiffened. She felt their hearts beating under the backs of her fingers.

"You called me a shifter that does not want to be a shifter. That is not true. I don't know how to be anything but what I am. However, I have no wish to be used as a power symbol for your thrones. I'm well aware of how rare my gifts are. I don't want the attention they'll bring."

"But you are amazing," William said.

"And rare," Douglas added.

"I know. I'm a collectable," she mumbled sarcastically. She began to sit up but Douglas held her hand to keep her down.

William placed his hand on her shoulder and turned on his side to face her. His breath tenderly hit her neck. "That is not how we see you. You're not some prize to be collected. We do see you for you, Rachel. Please believe that."

"You were right about one thing though," she admitted. "I don't like being the center of attention. I don't like the limelight, and I don't want the attention that being queen will bring. So, I thank you for your unasked but intended offer, but I have to be clear that I will decline. It would be foolish of me to leave here before whoever is trying to kill me is stopped, but after that, I want to go home to America. I'll run the sanctuary and dream of the days I spent with you both, but I don't want to be queen. I don't want to be torn between two clans. I don't want the peace, and lives, of every shifter on the planet to depend on my ability to make sure you two don't try to kill each other."

"Is this because we fought?" William asked. He touched her cheek, stroking it as if she might try to leave them that second.

"It wasn't even a fight, not really," Douglas said. "It was more like a heated discussion that needed to be said."

"We can do better," William assured her.

"Much better," Douglas agreed.

"It has nothing to do with your argument. In fact, now that I think about it, it was kind of hot to watch." She gave a small laugh, hoping to make them smile. They didn't.

"Then what?" Douglas put a hand along her waist.

"I don't want to live my life in politics, going from one clan to the other, from house to house, from life to life, having people count my days with one of you and feeling slighted if they're not even. If it was just us, just the three of us in our own special arrangement, then…" Her voice trailed off. Everything she was saying made logical sense, but her words were not convincing her heart. She had to be logical and reasonable. She knew herself, had purposefully hidden her true shifter gifts from the world. When she married, she wanted it to be for love, pure and simple love, not her omni-shifting abilities or politics, or to save two husbands from themselves.

"Then you would have us?" William prompted. "You would say yes to marriage?"

"We cannot change who we are. We have responsibilities to our people," Douglas asserted, as if the words were for William as well, a reminder that he had duties.

"No, we can do this. We can make our own arrangement, one that works for us," William insisted. "We'll build an estate on the border and live together so no one will be counting the days. The new address will be the perfect excuse to rein-vent our paperwork for the human records anyway."

"I own land that would be perfect for a house," Douglas offered. "There is a small home there already. It's older but will suffice while another is being built." He turned to Rachel. "And the politics are not so bad. You can do a lot of good. You will have the resources to take on whatever project you like."

"The limelight is tolerable once you get used to it. I had a hard time with it at first. To tell you the truth, at times it still bothers me, but we can face it together." William leaned up on an elbow to study her face. "You have no reason to worry. The people will love you."

"There are times I do not enjoy the attention," Douglas said. "And I will do all in my power to keep you from it, if that is your wish. Just, don't say no without thinking of our proposal. We will make you fine and honest husbands."

"Can't we…" Rachel wanted to say yes with the very beat of her heart, but her head was harder to convince. "Can't we just live in sin, together, as lovers? Do you really have to get married right away? You are here with me, so I'm assuming you have no prospects."

They didn't speak.

"Unless you do have other prospects? Magda gave you that list of potential brides you were reading before our car accident, didn't she? I heard her talking about Lisbetha. Well, *talking* is putting it mildly. She was actually mumbling about my apparent ineptitude and how poorly I was suited to be in your royal presence when there were much more suitable and aristocratic women around for you to pick from. Plus, she did try to send me through the servants' entrance. Then she had Lisbetha deliver my food like she was the lady of the house or something. She was in my room all of thirty seconds, but talk about uncomfortable."

Again, they didn't speak.

"If she is an example of how the people will love me, I think you've lost your argument. That woman has not liked me from the beginning. You'd think I marked her favorite tree during a shift or something." Rachel gave a small laugh, trying to lighten the mood, as she darkly joked, "I wouldn't be surprised if she was the one who hired St. Joan to come after me. She seems to have her nose stuck into every piece of business in this place."

The comment was meant to be more offhand than serious, but the second she said it, she felt Douglas inhale a deep breath and hold it.

"The idea does warrant looking into. Magda has been pushing for a Cononious bride," Douglas reasoned. "She's sent me a list of eligible women as well. In fact, I think she had Lisbetha's name starred, as well as the ones called Charity and Ginger. I believe the exact notation read, 'Ginger is wild and will most likely be to the Duncanis's liking'."

"I have known Magda since boyhood. She would not dare to betray me or our people." William sat up on the bed. Rachel studied his naked back as he presented it to them. His breathing stayed calm and even.

"What if she thought getting rid of me so you would marry a Cononious woman was in your best interest?" Rachel asked. "I'm Duncanis. She would have no reason to be loyal to me. It's clear she thinks of me as your American whore. She's given that impression since I've met her."

"No. I can't believe it. I couldn't accuse Magda of..." William's words trailed off. "If it is true, I will deal with her."

Rachel didn't know what to say. The men were quiet for a long moment.

"We don't know anything for sure." Rachel tried to backtrack her words, not liking the pain they clearly inflicted on William. "Our not knowing is merely leading to speculation. We have no proof."

"So are we to wait around for another attack?" Douglas asked. Rachel didn't like the idea of being bait. "I think we should question Magda. She would have the contacts, the knowledge, and the power to hire St. Joan."

"She is the one who told me who St. Joan was to begin with," William said, reluctantly. "I don't want to believe she would betray me, but the circumstances are suspicious. I will question her."

"This is a serious matter." Douglas pushed up. "I will be there when you question her. We will have a united front."

Both men looked expectantly at Rachel. She gave them a weak smile. "You two let me know how it goes."

"You should be there. This is your life that is being threatened," Douglas said. "And it will show our support of you if it is her."

"And your support of us," William added. "Like Douglas said, it is important that we be a united front."

"You two really do sound like politicians," she mumbled. Rachel moved to crawl out of bed. In all honesty, she didn't want to face Magda and see the old shifter eyeing her like she was a piece of gum stuck to her favorite table top. She lifted the cotton shirt and pulled it over her head.

"That is not an answer," Douglas said.

"I didn't really hear a question in the decree," Rachel answered. Now that her physical lust had been sated, her mind demanded a little more control. Her words seemed to quiet them. "Now, if you wouldn't mind picking up your clothes on your way out the door, I would like to be alone."

They shared a shocked look. William gave a short laugh, as if testing to see if she was joking.

"Oh, I'm serious. You two need to go and I need time to think." She grabbed her pants and held them in front of her, covering her naked bottom half from view.

"You won't run again?" Douglas asked as both men slowly got up from the bed.

"Not if you leave me in peace." Rachel was no fool. She didn't want to risk being drugged, kidnapped, hunted or killed. This room was the safest place at the moment. It would be even safer when the two incredibly handsome men left it. Then she would be somewhat protected from her own wayward emotions.

They dressed before leaving the room. Once alone, Rachel dropped her pants onto the floor and crawled half-dressed onto the bed. The covers smelled like them—the exotic cologne of Douglas and the wild earthiness of William. With a heavy sigh, she looked at the ceiling, but no revelations as to her situation came to her, and she was left feeling more confused than ever.

TWENTY-EIGHT

"My chief, the tailor is here to see to your fitting." Lisbetha curtseyed.

William nodded once in acknowledgement, only to stop walking and ask, "What? Tailor?"

After Rachel's dismissal and the others' suspicion about Magda, he had wanted to be alone to think. Seeing Lisbetha roaming the halls of his private wing caused him a moment's irritation until he reminded himself that it was his duty to be pleasant to the guests in his home.

"For the ball. Magda asked me to see to the details since you don't currently have a woman to care for such needs." Her smile was all innocence. "It is the same tailor my father uses, but don't worry, he does do more modern tuxedo styles as well."

William cleared his throat. "That was very, uh, thoughtful of you."

"It is nothing more than any lady would think to do." Again she smiled. Lisbetha was a very pretty woman, with clear eyes and immaculate hair. He found himself absently wondering how long it took a team of maids to get every strand into perfect place. "Ah." She made a weak noise, patting her hair.

William realized he stared. "Was there something else?"

"Only…" Lisbetha lowered her gaze only to peek up at him through her lashes. "Magda mentioned that you did not have a lady to take with you to the ball, and since I was effectively the hostess, I should make myself available to you for the evening."

"Oh." He glanced around the hall, more irritated at Magda for sending this woman to him— yet again. "I don't think it's necessary to trouble yourself."

"It is no trouble, my chief. I would be honored to sit by your side." Again when she smiled, the look was all innocence and purity. He almost felt bad telling her no.

"I'm sorry, but I have already made arrangements to have a woman by my side at the ball." William thought of his fiery Rachel. He wanted no other woman next to him. "Thank you for the offer, but it is not necessary."

Lisbetha's eyes narrowed. When he would step past her to avoid an awkward scene, she asked, "Might I ask who, my chief?"

"Rachel Dunne."

"The American trout?" Her words became tight.

William nodded. "Yes."

"But she is so…" Lisbetha made a disgusted noise. William arched a brow. The woman quickly checked her expression of distaste, and amended, "She is surely still recovering from her ordeal. Rumors have been circulating the castle that she was attacked by a wild dog when running alone in the forest. I, of course, have nothing against her, but people do speak of her…"

"Her…?" William prompted with a scowl. Who was this woman to lecture him about his choice in company?

"Her lack of propriety, that is all. I am sure it is only that she was raised wild in America." Lisbetha kept her expression docile. Except for the one slip of mild distaste she had briefly shown him, she hid her emotions well under the veiled mask of propriety. "Her nature cannot be helped. People also say that it is good of you to protect the poor orphan."

Orphan? Rachel wasn't some child in need of adopting.

"I especially think that is noble of someone to help the less fortunate. You have a good soul, my chief." Lisbetha dared to touch his arm. He looked down at her hand but didn't pull away. "If you change your mind and require a lady at your side, I will leave my evening open for you."

William nodded once. She curtseyed again and let her fingers trail off his arm before walking away. Her steps were small and unhurried. He listened until they were gone from his wing.

He hated palace gossip. It was no wonder Rachel wanted nothing to do with this life. He couldn't blame her. But yet, he couldn't let her go either. He made the sacrifice and gave up his anonymity when he became heir to Tobias's throne. Was it too much to ask that she made the sacrifice too? With her in his life maybe things wouldn't seem so lonely.

There was logic to a choice like Lisbetha, but he didn't want a cold marriage. He already had to share his bride with Douglas. It wasn't too much to ask that he actually desire the woman.

Frowning, he heard footsteps approaching. The gait sounded like Magda. In no mood to deal with the woman's lectures, and having agreed to confront the woman when Douglas was present,

William ducked into the old king's game room. He had not changed it since his ascension. The red pool table, billiards table, and air hockey tables dominated the room. The smell of old brandy and cigars hung lightly on the air.

He didn't move as he heard Magda walk by. She searched his bedroom before turning back around and moving down the hall, out of his private wing. Instead of leaving the room, he went to the bar and poured himself a snifter of Armagnac, a distinct smelling brandy from Gascony. It was the same drink Tobias had on his breath when he told William the news of his destiny as chief. William breathed in the scent, not tasting the drink for a long time while he remembered a time before that fated moment when his life had been much simpler.

TWENTY-NINE

DOUGLAS KNOCKED ON RACHEL'S BEDROOM door before walking inside uninvited. He found her sitting by the long window overlooking the back courtyard. Hours had passed since she'd asked to be alone, and he'd wanted to talk to her without William.

"I feel like I'm on vacation," she said wistfully, "aside from the someone wanting me dead part. That reality kind of puts a morbid spin on everything."

"I wanted to speak to you alone. I'm worried about your safety here. I think it would be best if you came with me to Scotland. There are many from the Duncanis clan there. They will welcome you because you are one of us. It is not like here. Those who work for me are not like Magda. You can trust them. We Duncanis protect our own." Douglas glanced towards the closed door. Rachel listened past him to what sounded like a maid in the halls. When she'd passed, he continued, "William is a good man. Tobias did right to choose him. However, he is new to his rule. There are some things—some instincts—that take time to develop. I have been chief for a long time and I trust my gut to know that it is not safe for us here."

"I have never been to Scotland." She looked out the window. Her solemn tone worried him. "Of course this is my first time in England too, and it is not how I would imagine such a trip. For one, I'd be here with a passport so I could go home."

"Rachel, for what it is worth, we are sorry about what has happened to you, but until we know why you were targeted, there is nothing to be done." He put his hands on his hips. "I apologize if this is insensitive, but it is time to act, not to wallow in self pity. I have a responsibility to keep you safe whether you are happy with my ways or not. The safest place for you right now is with me, in Scotland."

He half expected her to yell for his heavy-handed ways, but she surprised him. "What about

William? I will not leave without speaking to William."

"I would not ask you to, but we need to have a united front when we speak to him. He might not be able to come with us and he might not want to let you go. I know I wouldn't want to let you go." He ventured to move closer to her and brushed the hair from her face. "We should leave after the ball tomorrow night. Since William and I are forced to attend, you will need to be by our side so we can protect you. No one would dare attack in the crowd."

"I don't have a choice, do I?" She let loose a long sigh.

"Is it so bad?" he wondered aloud.

"What?"

"The idea of being with me, as my wife? Is it so bad?" With her he felt vulnerable. She was everything he wanted in a woman, and she could be his if she would just accept what was between them.

"But I would not just be with you."

"Of course, William as well. Are we so bad of a fate? Our lives have forced us to come to terms with the idea of sharing a wife, but is the idea of being our bride so horrible? Is it because William attacked you? Is it because I was not fast enough to stop him?"

"I meant it would not just be the both of you that I would be accepting. I would be taking on the whole shifter population." She took a deep breath. "It is not a responsibility I can accept lightly. My whole life I've hidden from what I am. Do you have any idea what it is like being an omni-shifter and not being able to tell people? Only a few people knew of it and they took it to their graves. Now you're asking me to announce it to the world. Marriage is a big step on its own, but this situation is complicated."

"Those are details that will work themselves out in time. What I feel for you. What William feels for you. Those things are not complicated. We're not humans, Rachel. When we meet our future, we know. I knew the moment I saw you in the bookstore that I wanted you."

"That's lust," she interjected with a small laugh.

"No, that was real. One look and you shot right through me. Before I even met you, I snapped your picture and sent it to William. It must have shot through him too, because he was on a plane to America just to get a glimpse of what could be. One picture is all it took and he was hooked." Douglas reached for her shoulders, pulling to urge her gently to her feet. "Don't make us spend eternity with a fill-in wife. That is a long time to ask us to be without you."

A tear pooled along her bottom lid. "Douglas—"

"Tell me you didn't feel our connection. Tell me when you were in the woods with us, just the three of us, you didn't feel the possibility of what we could be to each other."

"Of course I felt it. I felt it so strong it scared me, and I flew out of the second story window to run away from it." She wiped at her eye.

"Then—"

"I have heard what you have to say, but I won't make any decision until I hear what William has to say about all this. Scotland, balls, marriage, killers, there is a lot to think about." She touched his face. "But thank you, Douglas. Thank you for your sweet words, and your concern, and your—"

"Love," he stated. "You have my love."

"Yes, thank you for your love." She leaned into him, turning her mouth in invitation. "And I love you too."

It was all he needed to hear. Douglas leaned over and kissed her. The sweet taste of her lips washed over him. This was what he wanted—these tender private moments with Rachel. He accepted the arrangement of sharing her so long as it meant he got to have her. William was a good man, someone he would even call a friend. When he leaned in to kiss her, she lifted her fingers to his mouth to stop him.

"Yes, I feel it," Rachel said, "but I will not make a mindless decision with my heart. My brain has to be agreed or any life I have will be plagued with constant doubts and worry. This isn't some Hollywood movie where people ride off into the sunset happily ever after. This is real life and I won't give myself over to the idea unless I know heart and mind that I can be in one hundred percent. If I can't, there is no way I will be able to handle the pressure of the kind of spotlight life you live."

"I understand. I would want you to be sure. Tell me how I can alleviate your worry and—"

"Time to think," Rachel broke in. "I just need to time to think about such a big decision."

He didn't want to, but he nodded in agreement. Douglas pulled back from her. "Very well. I will give you the time you ask for."

When he let go of her to leave her alone, her hand on his arm stopped him. She gave a small smile. "I didn't mean this exact instant."

Douglas took the invitation and moved to kiss her. This time she didn't stop him as her lips met his and instantly parted. Their tongues rubbed slowly together in an erotically charged dance.

Rachel glided her hands onto his waist, lifting his shirt to discover the flesh beneath. Her gentle touch set his body on fire with need. Everything about this woman was sweet and perfect, and he had no doubt, given time, she would agree to be his bride. The very idea of not having her in his life was impossible to fathom.

Sweet caresses slowly became more fevered. He stripped her of her clothing so she stood naked before him in front of the window. The soft light embraced her.

Rachel's fingers fumbled with his pants as she tried to unbuckle his belt. He moved to help her, deftly unfastening the buckle. Her hand moved down the front of his pants over the material of his boxers, rubbing his erection through the fitted cotton. He moaned as she stroked him. The friction of her touch warmed his already hot member.

Aggressively, Douglas walked her back into the wall. He pushed his pants off his hips and pulled his boxers off his cock. The tighter material hugged his thighs. He growled in the back of his throat as he lifted her up. Her back pressed into the wall next to the window. If someone walked by on the ground below at the right angle, they would get a glimpse of the naughty couple. Douglas didn't care who saw. All he knew was he wanted to claim his woman—now and forever.

Holding her by her thighs, he entered her hard and sure. She accepted him and he let loose a small cry of victory. His hips began to pump. His body strained. Each thrust held within it a beautiful torment as he built towards a magnificent release. The rougher sex wasn't normally his style, but he couldn't slow. The jerking of his body was inelegant and raw. He didn't care. It felt too good, too right.

The second her body began to tremble in release, he let go. He came inside her, wanting to fill her with himself. When he looked into her eyes, he felt their connection and knew this was a woman he could spend the rest of his very long life loving.

THIRTY

DOUGLAS FELT THE PLEASURE OF RELEASE singing in his veins. If he could have, he would have spent the entire day with Rachel. However, he wanted to check with his guards and probe the palace servants to see if there were any suspicious people around, or at least people with suspicious behaviors. Though he wanted to spend every second with Rachel, he needed to make sure she was safe first.

After questioning several maids, some with intimidation and others with charm, he discovered quite a bit. One was fairly certain another was stealing food from the pantry to take home. Another believed the butler and the cook were having an affair. Yet another thought Ginger and Faith were having an affair with the same gardener. Lisbetha liked her meat raw because she believed it helped her complexion. Charity was fasting before the ball to fit into her sister's old gown. Magda was a well respected bitch who ruled the staff with an iron fist and little praise. Unfortunately, all their gossiping and information was completely irrelevant to him.

Seeing Lisbetha approach, he stopped. The woman seemed polite enough when he had the occasion to speak to her, but she was too boring for his tastes. He hated the niceties of English court life. He wanted his wild moorlands.

Lisbetha curtseyed. "Chief Duncanis, the tailor is here to see to your fitting."

"I have no fitting scheduled," he told her. Douglas thought about dismissing her, but decided he might as well see what she had to say about the people in the manor home.

"I apologize, but I took the liberty on your behalf. Since the ball was planned so suddenly, and you arrived with little by way of luggage, I thought you might require a tux." She coquettishly batted her lashes at him. "Magda asked me to see to the details since you don't currently have a wife to see to such needs."

"Magda asked you?" Douglas repeated.

Lisbetha nodded. "Yes. I have run my father's home for years now while he is away. The tailor is quite well trained. I have used him to make my father's suits over the years when he comes home. I took the liberty of guessing your size, so the fitting should not take long at all."

"Send him to my room. I will meet him there." Douglas hadn't given much thought to what he would wear to the ball. Normally, he did have trunks of luggage with him when he arrived at the English court. "And thank you for the kindness."

Lisbetha nodded. "There was one more thing, Chief."

"Yes?"

"Magda mentioned that you did not have a lady to take with you to the ball, and since I was effectively the hostess of the event I should make myself available to you for the evening."

"I have a date," he said.

"Oh?" She bit her lip and looked at the floor.

He felt kind of bad about her hurt feelings, and added, "Thanks for the thought, though."

"Might I guess that you will be bringing the American, as well?"

"As well?"

"My chief said he was taking Rachel Dunne to the ball."

Douglas nodded. "You know our traditions. It

is only natural that we should attend with the same woman."

"I see. I just thought since you weren't married, you might not be inclined to share. She is, after all…" She waved her hand dismissively before he could answer. "But it is not my place to speak out of turn about the American woman. If you change your mind and require a lady at your side, I will leave my evening open for you."

"What were you going to say?" Douglas demanded.

"Only that Miss Dunne is…" She hesitated. "It is not my place."

"Make it your place," he ordered.

"There are rumors about her. I don't normally like to repeat such things," again she hesitated, "and I'm sure you, Chief, being the informed man you are, already know what is being said."

"Tell me."

"Rumors have been circulating the castle that she was attacked by a wild dog when running alone in the forest. I, of course, have nothing against her, but people do speak of her lack of propriety. I am sure she is simply recovering from the ordeal and that is why she hides in the guest room. You can't believe she purposefully means to slight every person in the place."

Douglas didn't move.

"Still, shifters can be hot-blooded and sensitive," she continued, "and it has given them quite a distaste of the woman. I suppose allowances must be made for the fact that she was raised wild in America. Her feral nature and lack of manners cannot be helped. None of this reflects on you, of course. People also say that it is good of you to protect the poor woman."

He hadn't heard any such rumors. However, being the foreign chief, it wasn't surprising no one mentioned ill words about his current lover to him.

"You are very protective, aren't you? It comes from being a strong leader. It is good of you to help the unfortunate American and show her some favor. I hear she doesn't have family, so I'm sure your generosity will do much to help her gain some support within the shifter community when she goes back to America. It must be hard being a common fish. Such nobility as you display now will surely be noted when it comes time for you to consider a real candidate to be your bride."

Her words stung but he could find no fault in their candid delivery or her clear expression. Lisbetha touched his arm. He automatically pulled back from her. He thought about telling the woman that he's already chosen Rachel to be his bride, and he could care less what the gossips at the English court thought of his decision. He refrained, but only out of respect for Rachel. She had asked him for time to think. The last thing he needed to do was confirm a marriage she was not ready to announce. First the ball to deal with the public, and then they would talk about a wedding.

Lisbetha looked down at her slighted hand and curled the fingers slightly. "I will do what you asked and send the tailor for you. Perhaps you can save me a dance when Miss Dunne is otherwise engaged, or if she doesn't know how." Lisbetha curtseyed quickly, saying, "Chief," by way of excusing herself. She hurriedly walked away from him, her feet shuffling in tiny steps.

Lisbetha was dismissed from his thoughts the second she disappeared, but her words were not. There was only one person he knew of in the English court who could have started those rumors and who would have something to gain by them—Magda. Rachel's heritage was largely unknown to everyone else.

Lisbetha's words, though annoying, renewed his suspicions about the Cononious woman. It was time someone put Magda into her place. If the Cononious chief was not in a position to do so because of clan politics, then the Duncanis would just have to do it for him.

THIRTY-ONE

"THERE YOU ARE," RACHEL SAID. "I WAS looking for you."

William glanced up from the pool table, but didn't drop his stick as he took his shot. The ball bumped the corner pocket and didn't go in. He stood. "Pool was never really my game."

"Mine either. The sports bar where I work…" she paused, "where I *worked*, had five tables in the back. I doubt they held my job for me. In fact, I should probably call and tell them I'm all right just in case any of them care. And while I'm thinking about it, I do have an apartment in the city. I need to make some kind of arrangement to ensure my landlord gets a rent check. I'd hate for him to evict me while I'm here. He wouldn't hesitate to sell off what little belongings I have left.

Furniture can be replaced, but some photos and old letters cannot."

"Use any phone in the house to call the bar," he offered. "Write down your landlord's information and I'll see to the rent myself. Once things are a little more settled here, you can decide how you wish to handle the apartment. I can have someone gather your things and ship them here for you."

"Thanks." Rachel nodded.

"You said you were looking for me?"

Rachel went to the wall and absently picked up a cue stick. She let it glide between her fingers. William stood back from the table, silently offering to let her shoot. Her shot clanked the balls together in a haphazard fashion. They scattered about but none went in. "I told you I don't play."

He leaned over to take his turn.

"Douglas thinks we should go to Scotland where it will be safer for me since people are trying to kill me here. I told him I would have to speak to you first." Rachel set her stick on the ground and leaned against it. "You could come with us."

"So you've decided?" William did not dwell on the fact the two of them had talked about it, alone, without him. If he did, it would only invite jealousy.

"No. I've come to talk to you for your opinion." Rachel put the cue stick back on the rack and moved to lean against the table next to him. "I want to know what you think about it."

"Logically, I can see his reasoning. I would do anything to keep you safe." William stepped back and leaned his stick against the wall before resuming his position by her. "However, illogically, I don't want you to go. I want you to stay here with me."

"Can't you come with us?"

"Not until the matter of your safety is settled, and definitely not until after the ball. It would be ill advised for me to invite half the supernatural world, only to leave." He touched her face and gave her a soft smile.

"Ugh, I hate this," she complained, drawing her face from his touch. "I don't want to leave you behind. I don't want Douglas to leave without us. I hate the idea of having to split myself between two kingdoms."

William frowned, confused and worried. "What are you saying?"

"I'm saying I love you both and I don't like the situation we have found ourselves in. And I definitely don't love the idea of being forced to mediate between the two men I want to be with. I don't want to have to choose whether to stay or go." She sighed and her tone lost some of its ire, as she said, "I love you, William, and I want to hear what you think."

"I know that I love you too, Rachel." His heart beat happily in his chest as he leaned down to sprinkle kisses on her face. "And I think that nothing else matters. The rest are just details to be figured out."

"Those details are important, though. I will tell you like I told Douglas," Rachel inserted, when he would kiss her lips. She pushed on his shoulder to hold him back. "I will not make a mindless decision to marry both of you and to be queen of all shifters with just my heart. It's not a question of my love for you both, or my desire for you, because let's face it—I *always* want you. My problem is that my brain keeps coming up with very logical arguments as to why this is a bad idea. I don't want to be plagued with constant doubts and worry that I will not be able to stand the bright spotlight put on such a life. Plus, there is a very real chance the people won't want me to lead them. Already someone wants me dead, and I have a very hard time believing that it has anything to do with my very boring life in Colorado as owner of an out-of-commission shifter sanctuary."

"What can I do to convince you?" He gave a

very boyish grin, the kind of charming look men gave when they wanted something.

"Agree not to talk about it until after the death threat is taken care of." She ran her hand up his neck to his face. "And kiss me."

William did not have to be asked again. He moved his lips to hers, slowly kissing her with all the passion in his heart. He respected Rachel's logic, even as he knew in the end her arguments against being their queen would crumble. He couldn't blame her for being scared. At the sanctuary in Colorado, he'd seen the sheltered privacy of her life. To be taken from that into his world with such ferocity would shake anyone to the core. Yet, she didn't break down, didn't cry or whine. She stood strong, just like a true chieftess.

William knew that they would be safe in his private wing. He let his guard down as he lifted her by her hips and set her on the pool table. Her legs parted and he stood between them. Their kiss deepened. The sweet taste of her mouth caused him to moan.

"I love you, Rachel," he whispered against her lips. "Oh, I love you."

She grinned, pulling her shirt over her head. William unbuttoned her pants and tugged them off her hips when she lifted up off the table. He unbuttoned his shirt and let it drop behind him. Her hands glided over his chest and shoulders, exploring everywhere she could reach as he unfastened his belt.

When his pants dropped to his ankles, he brought himself forward. The heavy length of his erection found its aim. He entered her slowly, moaning at the soft way her moist flesh caressed and held him.

Rachel rolled back onto the pool table. William remained on his feet. He held her hips angled towards him, watching her naked body move as they made love. Her arms hit the pool balls and their soft clanks sounded over them. As she came, her body tensed. The beauty of the moment was too much and he found his release inside her.

Rachel gave a small, happy laugh before moaning. She smiled up at him, her gaze clear and bright. Her laughter rose as she turned her hip. He let go of her legs. She reached down to where her ass cheek pressed into the table and pulled out a piece of pool cue chalk. When he looked, there was a blue, small square imprinted on her flesh.

"Maybe next time we find a bed," she said, reaching her hand up to him so he could help her up.

THIRTY-TWO

"I KNOW IT WAS YOU, MAGDA," DOUGLAS stated. He had the old shifter cornered in the library. She clutched a clipboard to her chest, her knuckles white, but otherwise did not show any emotion on her cold demeanor. "My father warned me about you and your disrespect. He said to watch you closely when Tobias died. I see his suspicions about you were well founded."

"I am sure I don't know what you mean, Duncanis." Magda lifted her chin. Her dress suit was immaculately pressed and her hair swept back into a very stark, serviceable bun.

"You hired St. Joan to kill Rachel in America. You handle William's travel arrangements and you knew why he was traveling to the US and where he would be. You had no way of knowing he would arrive at the cabin early. You arranged transportation when the plane touched down. You told St. Joan and her leopard cohort where to find us. Nothing happens in this place without your knowing about it. You knew Rachel went for a run and you probably knew William went after her. That is why you did not tell me they were missing. You gave St. Joan time to get away." Douglas's entire body was stiff and he felt the beast inside him threatening to come out. "It is you who has been spreading the rumors around the manor about her heritage, trying to undermine her any way you can think of."

"Those are strong accusations, Duncanis. Where is your proof?" Magda pressed the clipboard tight to her chest. When he didn't readily supply it, she continued, "I thought so. You have no proof because there is none. I have been a loyal member of my clan my entire life, not that a Duncanis would know much about loyalty."

"Loyal? How is kidnapping your own chief showing loyalty?" Douglas demanded. "If this was my court you would be strung up in the yard. That is what happens to traitors."

"Then it is a good thing I don't belong to your rash clan." Magda slammed the clipboard down on the table. "I have heard quite enough. William may be a young chief, but he is still my chief. He will not stand for your accusations against me. If he thought as you do, he would be here with you."

"I do not need William by my side to act."

"You do if you want to accuse one of his top people of being a traitor." Magda lifted her jaw. She tried to walk past him. Douglas grabbed her arm. She stood tall and looked at his hand on her. "What do you think you're going to do? Kill me? Here? While a guest in this house? With high-powered guests arriving in hours for the ball?"

Douglas released her arm. He didn't want to. He wanted to throw her out the window. Magda marched from the room. Douglas went to her discarded clipboard and looked over the papers. They were purchase orders for the kitchens and lists of supplies for the ball. He set it back down. It was hardly the nefarious evidence he needed.

Even as he confronted the woman, he knew he should have waited for William. The anger had just built after hearing Lisbetha's rumors. All the frustration he'd felt when Rachel was gone, combined with his desperation to keep her safe now, had just been too much to resist.

THIRTY-THREE

"I HAVE NEVER BEEN DISLOYAL TO MY CLAN!"

Rachel ducked back into the hall at the sound of Magda's voice. Magda was the last person she wanted to run into—especially smelling of William and wearing his clothes. Rachel had left the game room to steal one of William's shirts from his bedroom. By a turn of bad luck, or at least an amusing consequence, her shirt had found its way into William's brandy snifter while they had sex.

"The Duncanis chief has his reasons to be suspicious of you. You must admit your behavior regarding Rachel has been suspect." William's voice was calm compared to Magda's.

"Of course I think it would be better with the

American out of the way!" Magda returned. "She shows no respect. She's wild. She is a Duncanis."

"But to order her death?" William asked.

Rachel edged closer to the door and leaned in, though really with her hearing she didn't need the advantage.

"You think I am a traitor?" Magda asked, her tone somewhere between outrage and hurt. "You think as the Duncanis chief does?"

"I don't know what to think."

"You know me."

"Yes," William agreed in irritation, "I do know you, Magda. That is part of the problem. I know you would do anything you thought was right for our clan. I know you hate anyone who isn't Cononious, and secondarily anyone who is not English. I know you have been shoving English Cononious females in my face since the second of my accession to chief. You knew we were in America. You knew *where* in America. We told no one else about it. You saw the picture Douglas sent me of Rachel before I left. You knew we were interested in finding out if she was a suitable bridal candidate before I even went there. Who else had that information?"

Rachel stiffened. They tracked her down? Their meeting was on purpose? Planned? Douglas had already told her about the picture he'd sent, but somehow when William talked about it to Magda, it seemed so much colder and more deliberate.

William continued, "I didn't want to believe it, but then after our return from the forest you came to my room acting not like yourself. There was something strange in your tone, Magda, just as there is something strange in your expression now."

"You take the word of the Duncanis over your own?" Magda's voice dropped.

"I take my own logic. Like it or not, Magda, I choose Rachel. Douglas chooses Rachel. There is nothing you can do to stop our upcoming wedding. She will be chieftess and if anything happens to her, I will make sure my next bride is a Duncanis from Australia with a well documented history from the prison colonies. I am sure the notorious mass-murdering shifter, Darius Drake, had children while banished there."

Magda gasped in horror. "You wouldn't! That wolf ran rampant over the civilized world. His children are outcasts! You would dare taint the royal bloodline?"

"I most definitely would. So decide, Magda, Rachel or a Drake?"

Rachel had heard stories of Darius Drake when she was little. They were scary bedtime stories warning shifters of what happened when they didn't obey the rules. Darius had been a feral wolf that terrorized Europe in the 1800s. When they caught him and he said he was a shifter, the humans instantly stamped him insane, drugged him, and carted him off to Australia's prison colonies. The details of the transfer were hazy, but she seemed to remember that shifters had been the ones to take him so his secret was never seen and shifters were not exposed. The werewolf murders had been big news at the time, second only to some of the vampire stories.

Rachel wasn't sure how she felt being compared to a Drake descendent. At least she was a step above crazy. She was still more disturbed that the two chiefs came to America specifically to judge her bridal suitability. How did she even get on their radar? Was it the omni-shifting? They had seemed genuinely surprised when she told them about it.

Magda asked. "Is that all?"

"No. Unfortunately your role here only works if I trust you. I don't trust you. The Duncanis does not trust you. I do not have proof of your crimes against us and that is the only reason you are not going to be severely punished. If proof does surface, then I will deal with you accordingly at that time. Call off the attacks, Magda. Whatever else you have planned, call it off."

"What will you do with me?" Magda whispered.

"I think it is time you retired. Officially, because of your years of service and loyalty, I will accept your retirement and gift you with the Southern cottage. You stay there, out of trouble, or unofficially I will have you dragged away in the middle of the night." William's tone lightened. "I am sorry it has come to this. You have been good to me over the years."

"Apparently not good enough," she said angrily.

"You may stay for the ball tonight and announce your retirement there. You will be watched, so don't try anything."

"Goodbye, my chief," she grumbled bitterly.

Rachel heard footsteps and pulled back down the hall. She wasn't quick enough. Magda saw her and stopped. Rachel opened her mouth but nothing came out. Rage burned in the other woman's normally composed gaze.

"The others will never fully accept you. If you think I'm the only one unhappy with this union, you are more foolish than I thought, little fish," Magda stated before storming down the hall, out of William's private wing.

Rachel didn't move. William quickly appeared through the door, glancing after Magda and then to Rachel. "I didn't hear you in the hall."

"You were distracted," Rachel answered. "So is that it? Is it over? Magda is banished and…"

"She should no longer be a threat to you." William came fully into the hallway. "She's not foolish. She'll call off any attack she has planned. The woman is politically motivated, not suicidal. I should have seen it earlier, I'm sorry. But whatever happens, we will keep you safe."

"So if it's over, I can go home now?" Rachel crossed her arms over her waist. Her stomach churned and her heartbeats felt heavy and raw.

"What do you mean?" William asked. "Home?"

She didn't meet his eyes. If she did, she would get lost in them just as she always did. "I know you targeted me. I know I'm the reason you were in Colorado. It wasn't a chance meeting. Douglas found me, sent you a picture, and you both came to check me out to see if I was marriage-worthy. It wasn't fate. It was politics." She hugged her arms tighter. The shirt she wore smelled of his laundry detergent. "I heard everything, William. Magda's right. She's not the only one who will oppose to me as a chieftess. I have said it from the beginning, what do I know of this life? I will go to the ball tonight because I promised you both I would. But then I want you to let me go home. I don't belong here. I belong running the Colorado sanctuary. That is my destiny. I think this whole crazy experience was to show me my place in the shifter world."

"You can't mean this," William stated.

"I can and I do." Rachel frowned. "I know you are listening, Douglas. You might as well join us. It will save me from having to repeat this later."

Douglas appeared down the hall. He walked slowly. His stricken expression found hers. "You can't leave."

"And you can't make me stay," she countered. Well, in truth, they could. They were the most powerful shifters in the world. "I don't know how you knew about my abilities, but that is the only reason I can think of that you would come to America to find me."

"I went to America to find a bride who was not politically motivated to be with us," Douglas said.

"That does not make it sound any better," she answered. Somehow, she'd convinced herself that their joining was fate. What a silly notion, fate. This circumstance was planned. They planned it for political reasons.

"We thought you were a trout," Douglas said, "and we wanted you anyway."

"What he means is we do want you. We don't care what kind of shifter you are," William amended, trying to soften Douglas's bluntness.

"But it does help that you are strong. For that alone the people will accept you." Apparently, Douglas did not want his point to be softened.

"The fact we care for you will also persuade them." William tried to smile at her. His hand lifted briefly in her direction as if the gesture could draw her in. "Those who are resistant will come to accept you."

On one hand, here she had two very attractive, smart, sexy, powerful men practically on bended knee. On the other, she had a lifetime of Elvie's warnings, hippie teachings and self-doubts. Elvie would tell her to let the wild out. How could she do that as chieftess? Elvie would tell her to be careful, that she should never have let them see her gifts. She would warn about how the hundreds of years of single life could change. Today they might not experiment on her kind, but shifters had in the past and they might again in the future.

Her brain and her heart were not meeting eye to eye, and she didn't know which organ to trust. Was her heart foolish? Was her brain overthinking a very simple thing?

If the truth were known, she had thought she'd have more time to decide. When she'd told them both—mere hours before—that she loved them and would re-address the marriage thing when the threat had passed, she didn't expect the threat to be resolved so quickly.

"One of the maids said something about having a dress delivered to my room for tonight. I'm going to shower, nap, try it on, do other girl things." It was a lame excuse to get away from the two of them, but if she stayed there much longer her heart would take completely over, and she would give in to whatever they wanted.

"Be careful," William said. "You should be safe, but it's wise to be careful until Magda leaves."

Rachel nodded and moved away from them, not really focusing on her surroundings as much as she should have as she walked to her guest room.

❧

"Magda is leaving?" Douglas asked. "What happened?"

"I should ask you the same thing." William stared down the hall where Rachel had disap-peared. He wanted to go after her, but he had seen the look on her face. She was confused, hurt, mostly confused. "I thought we were going to confront Magda together."

"The moment came up and I took it," Douglas answered. "I was on my way here to tell you. It appears Magda found you first."

"Yes, I banished her with some stern threats. Legally, we can do little else without proof. I don't think she will cause problems. At this point, if something happened to Rachel, she knows she'd be blamed." William took a deep breath and motioned into the game room. "Care for a drink? It looks like we have some things to discuss."

Douglas nodded, following the man inside.

THIRTY-FOUR

THE BALL WAS EVERYTHING RACHEL IMAGINED A 19th century English manor gala would be, with the addition of vampires, fairies, witches, a goblin or two who apparently snuck in the servant's entrance to crash the event, what looked to be a pet troll brought in under a large, black blanket, and a handful of creatures she had no idea what to call. Candles burned over the hall, shining over the crush of bodies filtering through the main entryway. Fresh cut flowers scented the air by their sheer volume, and their large, crystal vases sparkled like stars around the edges of the dance floor. A live quartet played ballroom music. Rachel's dance experience was limited to country line dancing and techno bobbing in dark clubs.

Jumping up and down at a high school rave hardly prepared her for something like this.

In what Rachel was sure was one of Magda's final jabs, the gown she'd been given to wear was one size too small and only buttoned up the back with the aid of a corset. It made it hard to breathe. Though ornate, with a flared skirt of purple tulle and ribbon, she thought the look better suited to the top of a wedding cake or in a ballet than on her body. Thankfully, though, she seemed to match the other ladies in attendance.

Who she didn't match was Douglas and William. Their tuxedos were dark and of the finest cut, complete with deep red accents that clashed with her ballerina purple. Still, she stood between them as their joint date and greeted all who entered the hall. She didn't have much to say to anyone, so she did her best to stand quietly and smile.

Magda did not show herself. Rachel wasn't sure if that was comforting or not.

As the last of the guests arrived, she was introduced to some of the residents of the manor. The sisters Faith, Hope and Charity were polite, and seemed to have little ill will towards her apparent position as what they termed "the chiefs' favorite". Judith was a dark, slender woman whose movements looked better suited to the ballerina outfit

Rachel wore. Then came the infamous Lisbetha and her less noticeable companion, Ginger. Ginger didn't stay long, as her eyes wandered off towards a group of young-looking vampire men in attendance with King Kristoff. For all Rachel knew, each vampire could have been centuries old. When she greeted the pale creatures, they had the distinct smell of dust beneath their heavy cologne.

Lisbetha, however, stood out from everyone in the crowd. Not only was she beautiful, but her sleek evening gown was the exact shade of red that accented the chiefs' tuxedos. Her blonde hair was piled on the top of her head and her makeup was flawless. When she took her place next to them, she looked like she belonged.

"I see my father's tailor did a stunning job. I chose very well," Lisbetha commented. The woman's ploy worked. Rachel felt like the outsider. Already she was uncomfortable in her tightly cinched gown, but now anyone who looked at the four of them would easily pick her as the odd one out.

"Rachel, would you honor me?" Douglas asked.

Rachel shook her head in denial. "I don't dance like this."

"We can show you," William whispered.

She eyed the couples on the dance floor. They

looked as if they had been doing the steps for centuries. There was no way she was going to let the chiefs take turns while she stepped on their toes and made a public ass out of herself.

"I would be honored to dance with you, my chief," Lisbetha said loudly as she looked up at William.

He glanced around. Several had heard the woman's decree, and he had little choice but to lead her to the dance floor.

Rachel resisted the urge to trip Lisbetha. She watched William lead the woman artfully in the dance steps. As jealous as she was, there was no way Rachel could even begin to mimic the movements. The combination of heat and a tight corset caused her to sway on her feet. A tiny bead of sweat worked its way down the back of her neck. She blinked, suddenly lightheaded.

"How long do I have to stay here?" Rachel asked Douglas.

"Rachel," Douglas whispered a little too harshly, as he grabbed her elbow.

"How long do I have to stay here?" she repeated. Her vision blurred. She heard a gasp and the music stopped.

"Why are you yelling?" Douglas asked in her ear. He tried to force her to walk but she couldn't pick up her feet.

"Yelling?" She frowned. "I don't feel right."

Suddenly, her body erupted with tingling sensations. It felt like a shift, but much stronger. She couldn't control it. Her body jerked and she suddenly flopped on the floor.

❖

DOUGLAS WATCHED, STUNNED, AS RACHEL'S arm turned into the hard, gray flesh of a shark fin. She slipped from his hand with a heavy thud to land on the floor. Her gown ripped as she thrashed her way out of it. Her body flopped across the hard marble. Her head and back fin made horrible flapping noises as they struck the floor and she snapped her jaw.

"A shark?!" Lisbetha screamed as Rachel flopped her way towards the woman. Some vampires laughed at the chaos of people running from the dance floor.

"Rachel." William tried to approach her, but she didn't seem to recognize him.

"Water!" Douglas ordered. "We need water."

"She said that she had swum in the ocean," William said. He pointed at some servants with food trays. "Salt water. From the big aquarium in the library."

The servants slid their trays onto a nearby

table and hurried to do as they were told. A few of the partygoers rushed outside, the stubby, little goblin party crashers leading the way. Rachel began to jerk violently.

"What's wrong with her?" Douglas hated feeling helpless.

The witch, Julianne, stepped forward. Her dark, smooth hair and olive complexion stood against the virginal white of her gown. Very calmly, she picked up Rachel's dress and sniffed it. She made a sour face and handed it to her twin sister, Bella. Bella inhaled deeply and licked the material.

"*Datura stramonium*," Julianna stated. "Jimson weed."

"Her gown is soaked with it," Bella confirmed. She licked it again before handing it back to her sister. "And shifter blood."

The servants came back with pitchers of salt water and tossed the contents on the floor towards Rachel. Their aim had little effect as it splashed across the marble. Rachel jerked again.

"William, help me grab her. We'll put her in the tank," Douglas said.

Before they could get a hold of her, she bucked off the ground and began to change again.

"Unpredictable stuff, the *Solanaceae* family," Julianna stated, calm in the chaos.

"Very powerful nightshade," Bella agreed. The two sisters continued to hand the dress back and forth, licking and smelling it.

"Who cares about her gown? She's rabid!" Lisbetha yelled. "Someone stop her before she kills us all!"

Rachel's body grew smaller. Each second ticked by in agonizing slowness as if her body couldn't decide on what form it wanted to be. Every time they tried to touch her, her tremors became violent.

"Don't touch her," Julianna said.

"It will make the distress worse," Bella added. "Her body will think it's under attack."

"You two seem to know a lot about this," William stated, accusingly.

"That is very kind of you to say," Bella answered, smiling at the compliment.

"But this is hardly our work. We're voting for this one," Julianna said. "New blood on the shifter throne."

"What?" Lisbetha demanded. "New blood? Are you serious? Look at her! She's a freak."

As if to answer, Rachel burst off the floor and into the air. She flew high into the ceiling.

"Omni," someone whispered, only to be repeated several times.

"I like this one!" a vampire yelled. "She's entertaining. Not the usual stuffy princesses you guys marry."

"What?" Lisbetha screamed. "No!"

Rachel circled overhead. William pushed his way into the crowd, following her as if he would catch her when she fell.

Douglas turned his attention to the sister witches. "What else can you tell me? Who did this?"

"It's an old recipe, but not too old. Jimson weed was originally found in the Americas. Maybe 1600s," Julianna answered.

"Old family magic," Bella added. "This is not a commercial blend. No one uses blood anymore. Too unsanitary. Too unpredictable."

"Some do," Julianna countered.

"Well, yeah, some." Bella gave a look of distaste as the sisters shared a private moment.

Rachel cried out, the kind of noise a bird of prey made before they attacked. She swooped towards the crowd. The vampires clapped and shouted. Other creatures ducked and scurried out of the way.

"Some help," William yelled up at tiny fairies. They didn't seem to mind the bird as they flew after it, more playful than trying to actually capture Rachel. Their buzzing laughter rained down over those below.

Douglas noticed Magda in the doorway, looking up at the ceiling. Just as he was about to charge at her and demand justice, she turned to look at Lisbetha. Her eyes narrowed on the woman and she charged forward.

Rachel screeched again. Suddenly, she stopped flying and dropped. The fairies behind her scattered. William dove to catch her. Her wolf body fell against him and took him to the ground. They slid on the wet floor into the wall. Now, deadlier than before, she snarled. William held on tight. Douglas dove forward to help subdue her. Rachel's teeth caught William's shoulder. He cried out but didn't let go. His blood smeared on the marble as they fought to control her. Damn, but Rachel was strong.

"What did you do?" Magda yelled. Douglas tried to look, but couldn't take his eyes off Rachel.

"Whatever do you mean?" Lisbetha asked in affront. "I'm sure I don't know what you're talking—"

"Shut it!" Magda yelled. "I have evidence of you breaking into my room."

"What? No, that's not possible." Lisbetha gave a nervous laugh.

"I have you recorded. I always keep my security on," said Magda.

"Best ball ever," a vampire declared, only to be shushed by his companions.

"It's not what you think," Lisbetha said.

"The guards searched your room. We found the cauldron under your bed. Now what did you do?"

"Jimson weed," Bella supplied, happy to infuse the situation. "A potion to cause uncontrolled shifting."

"No, no, shut up, you hag!" Lisbetha yelled. "That wasn't me. I just gave the American something to make her doubt herself, and her feelings, just a little Doubting Thomas in her food. Just a small amount. That's all. I was only doing what you and everyone here wanted. I just wanted her to go home."

"Lies, lies," Bella chanted. "You don't need a cauldron for that potion."

"Please, let us talk about this elsewhere," Lisbetha insisted. She backed away from the crowd, shaking her head in denial. "Magda, you know me. I'm a lady. I couldn't do this."

Rachel growled low in the throat. Douglas and William held on tight. She lost a bit of her struggle.

"Your shoulder?" Douglas asked William when he winced.

"Fine," William answered, though clearly the wound was bleeding profusely. He gave a small, humorless laugh, and mumbled, "Right now I almost prefer she was a trout."

Douglas chuckled and held on tighter as Rachel tried to throw them off her. He drew his head back, barely missing the snap of her jaws as she tried to take off his nose.

"I know your family has connections to the late Mr. St. Joan," Magda said.

"So do a lot of families. That stupid little uprising was a long time ago." Lisbetha gave a little dismissive laugh. No one joined her.

"Guards," Magda ordered. "Take Lisbetha Rue into custody for treason against our clan, and against the future chieftess of the shifters."

Though it wasn't much of a surprise, this was the first time any official announcement had been made. The gathering cheered, despite the current state of the future shifter queen and the chaos of the dance floor.

"Treason? No! I am a lady. I deserve to be queen. I did everything you asked of me, Magda! Everything!"

"I never asked you to betray our people," Magda defended. "Guards, take her!"

As the shifter guards made a move to go through the crowd, Lisbetha screamed. She reached for her skirt, lifting it as she ran towards Rachel. When her hand withdrew from beneath the red material, she held a knife.

"None of this would have happened if you would have just died in America like you were supposed to!" With deadly precision, she threw the blade. Douglas pushed up from the floor, twisting Rachel out of the way. The knife struck his back. He cried out as the white-hot pain took hold of him.

"Help them," King Kristoff ordered. The young vampires who had been enjoying the show instantly obeyed. Fangs bared, they swarmed forward to help subdue the future shifter queen. Douglas let go as her weight pulled from him. He collapsed onto the floor.

"No," Lisbetha screamed, kicking as the guards forced her out of the room towards the prison hold below the manor. "I didn't do anything wrong!"

Douglas fought for concentration against blood loss. He heard Magda ordering that the lazy ass of a doctor be roused out of whatever drunken corner he'd fallen into. Kristoff ordered his vampires to help bring the angry queen to the safety of an iron cage.

THIRTY-FIVE

"WE LIKE YOU. YOU ARE STRONG."

Rachel blinked heavily before jerking her arm back from the witch who held it. She vaguely remembered meeting her at the ball, and her mind only recalled that much because she had an exact replica of a twin next to her. The "cursed sisters", Douglas had called them.

"And you are very hexed," the other twin added. Rachel couldn't tell them apart.

She was in a jail cell on a cot. Stone walls surrounded them. There were no windows, only fluorescent lights flickering overhead. What the hell happened?

"Am I under arrest?" Rachel asked. Even to her own ears her words were slurred.

The witches laughed. The one on the right

turned around and asked, "What all did you give her?"

Rachel sat up on the cot. For a prison, the mattress wasn't bad. She saw Lisbetha sitting in an adjoining cell, her red dress torn. At Rachel's attention, she glared.

Rachel leaned in to one of the witches, "Did I get into a drunken brawl?"

Again the sisters laughed.

"If we would have been allowed to brawl fairly, I would have won and you would be dead," Lisbetha hissed.

"Fair?" Magda appeared in the stone entry-way. "Doubting Thomas to create uncertainty. A tincture of human papillomavirus to give warts. Jimson weed in a blood spell to cause uncontrol-lable shifting—no doubt to expose her as a trout before the court. And payments from your father's account to St. Joan. I would hardly call the way you fight as being fair. Though, if the future queen would like, we can enact the old laws and let you two fight to the death. However, after seeing Lady Dunne's talents, I doubt you would want to accept such an offer."

Lisbetha looked pale and pressed her lips tight.

"I thought not, little bird." Magda turned her attention to Rachel. "I suppose we are in the sisters' debt now. They have taken very good care of you."

"No reason to sound so surprised," one of the sisters answered. "As we told you, we like this one."

"She smiled at us and took our hands without hesitation when we entered the hall," the other sister added. "Such kindness is rare from a shifter noble. She was not frightened by our curse." Then to Rachel, she said, "At your service, lady." Rachel smiled, confused but not wanting to hurt their feelings by admitting so much. The sisters stood. "Watch her for a few days. She'll be too weak to shift, but after that there should be no ill effects."

Magda opened the door to her cell and the sisters left. Rachel pushed weakly to her feet. The door was left open for her, letting her out.

"You are very lucky," Magda said. "I suppose there is some sign in that."

"I don't take you as someone who believes in signs." Rachel leaned against the prison bars, trying to catch her breath. She ached deep inside.

"I don't." Magda didn't offer her arm, but she did wait patiently.

"What exactly am I missing? You had Lisbetha poison me, but now changed your mind?" Rachel really hoped the older woman didn't attack. She wouldn't be able to defend herself.

"If my chief questioned my motives, it can only mean I failed to carry myself well. I regret that. However, I have always only acted in the best interest of my clan. Lisbetha acted alone. She hired St. Joan. She laced your gown with poison so that it would be activated by the heat of your body and absorbed through the skin."

Rachel looked to where Lisbetha sat quietly glaring at her.

"It is over. She will be punished." Magda glared back at the woman. "Her father is already being informed."

Lisbetha gasped and instantly shook her head in denial. "No, not my father. You can't—"

"It is done," Magda stated. She silently urged Rachel to walk beside her.

"You can't send me back to my father's keeping!" Lisbetha yelled.

"She's not going to be...?" Rachel glanced back to Lisbetha who held tightly to the bars.

"Treason means either death or exile. Since you were not officially queen when she acted, it is exile. In this case, to her father's keeping. He is a gentleman scientist in the Amazon. For a lady of the court, it is as far from civilization as we can send her. If she comes back to Europe, she will be killed."

"Magda." Rachel stopped and leaned against the wall outside the prison. The long, stone corridor was cool and led to a row of stone steps in the distance. She took a breath. "What happened? I don't remember anything after Lisbetha asked William to dance."

"After my anger cooled, I decided to check the footage from my private security camera I have hidden in my suite. It's a closed circuit, and Lisbetha could not know I set it up. When I saw her snooping through my computers and filing cabinet, I knew she was to blame. The guards checked her room and I checked her personal bank accounts." Magda quickly recounted what had happened at the ball, adding, "Lisbetha has always been ambitious, but I did not think her capable of this level of deceit. It is my fault she was able to access my room without suspicion. I have known William since he was a boy. I had my suspicions about why he was going to America, though he tried to hide them. Lisbetha read my notes and must have sent St. Joan to watch the mountain sanctuary—the most natural place for the chiefs to stay while trying to keep a low profile overseas. It was my decision to give her so many responsibilities and to put her forward as a candidate for royal marriage. Chief William is quite right to insist I retire."

If it had been anyone else, Rachel might have tried to say something comforting. Magda's expression did not welcome such sentiments. Instead, she said, "I'm sorry your loyalty was questioned."

"Thank you, lady," Magda answered. "Now, if you don't mind, I believe your presence with your grooms would be beneficial. The doctor has stitched them both up, but—"

"Where are they?" Rachel forced her sore legs to move up the stairs. She held onto the wall but didn't stop even as her muscles burned. Her heart beat in worry.

"Chief William's wing," Magda said.

It took all her energy, but the idea of William and Douglas in trouble propelled her forward. She should have known something was wrong when she woke up without them. No amount of duty would have kept them from her side. She was sure of that fact.

Her shoulder dragged against the wall as she neared William's room. She heard the low sound of voices inside and didn't bother knocking. Douglas lay on the bed, a bandage around his chest. William sat on a chair next to him, his shoulder completely covered in white gauze. At her entrance, they both made a move to get up.

"Don't you dare move," she ordered, limping towards the bed. Relief filled her to see them awake.

"Rachel," William said, "sorry we couldn't go to you and you had to wake up in a prison cell, but the sisters sent reports of their success. The cell was for your protection until the poison wore off."

"It's fine." Rachel held on to one of the bed posts for support. "How are you? What happened to you two? Magda said a doctor had been sent for?"

"You bit me," William said.

She pursed her lips together. "I don't remember…"

William gave her a small grin. "It was kind of sexy, so I don't mind. Plus, you owed me one. We're even."

"And you?" Rachel sat on the bed, too weak to stand.

When Douglas didn't answer, William said, "He took a knife meant for you."

"That is what Magda meant when she said Lisbetha tried to kill me tonight. I thought she meant the poison dress." To Douglas, she asked, "What did the doctor say?"

"To not get stabbed," Douglas answered wryly. "I will be fine. He ordered we both rest for a few days until we're well enough to shift."

Rachel touched his arm before making her way along the bed. She touched William as she passed him. "It's over, isn't it?"

"Yes," they both said at the same time.

"Good," she mumbled tiredly, "because I can think of only one thing I want to be doing right now."

Douglas grinned wickedly, even though his features were pale. She frowned. "Not that."

"But…" he protested.

"Sleep," Rachel said, crawling next to him on the bed. She left enough room on her other side for William to join them. She patted the bed and gave him a meaningful look. "Lots and lots of sleep. And I won't be able to rest unless we're all together."

William made his way slowly, gingerly lying next to her. She touched both of them, able to relax now that she was surrounded by the men she loved.

"But after we're healed…?" Douglas asked.

Rachel gave a short laugh as she closed her eyes. "Yes. After."

THIRTY-SIX

EPILOGUE

RACHEL LOOKED AT HER TWO HUSBANDS AND grinned. How could she have ever doubted her love for them? Even with the Doubting Thomas potion Lisbetha had used in her food, she should have known her heart. The very idea of not being with them caused an instant tear to choke her.

Lisbetha had been shipped off to her father in chains, completely disgraced and bitter. Though William apologized for his accusations and offered to let her stay in her current position, Magda insisted on retiring. She did not trust her own opinion after misjudging Lisbetha. The older woman did, however, offer to come back and be the caretaker of the future royal children. Rachel wasn't so sure about the idea.

"It's done," William said, handing a rolled

parchment to his contractor. The man left the royal trio alone. "They break ground on our new home immediately."

Rachel grinned. It was the only condition she'd had on marrying them. She wanted a joint home where they all lived together. She didn't want to split her time between the two men. She wanted a strong family unit. She wanted to raise her kids under one roof. She also wanted to join the clans in a way that didn't demand the sacrifice of a joint marriage. Though, seeing her current situation, she didn't think a joint marriage was so horrible. Still, one lucky, royal marriage did not make up for all the not-so-good ones that came before.

Rachel pushed up from the chair in William's study. Now that they were all three alone, she moved to sit by Douglas on a small couch. William instantly sat next to her. It was a tighter fit but none of them minded. Sighing in contentment, Rachel closed her eyes and said, "I do hope the house is done in time."

"In time for what?" Douglas asked absently as he stretched out his feet next to her. William angled his body so she fell against his chest. Douglas pulled her legs onto his lap, turning her. He rubbed her calf muscles.

"In time to start a family." She gave a soft smile and didn't move.

"Family?" William asked. His fingers skated absently along her arm.

"Don't tell me you both are really so dense? We've had sex how many times without protection?" Rachel chuckled.

It took the men a moment to react.

"Yes?" William asked, stiffening behind her.

"You are?" Douglas demanded, dropping her feet on the floor. He reached to touch her stomach.

Rachel nodded happily.

The men looked at each other in excitement and said in unison, "We're going to be fathers."

"We're going to need supplies," Douglas said. "Diapers. Milk. One of those jumping things that hangs from the doorway."

"We're going to need a bigger house," William countered. Rachel fell onto the seat as he abruptly stood. "I need to catch the contractor."

"But our house is already going to be huge," Rachel said, shocked as William ran from the room. To Douglas she began to speak, but he cut her off.

"I can't believe he's worried about the contractor at a time like this," Douglas said.

Rachel gave a short laugh. At least one of them was going to stay with her and celebrate.

"Especially when there are things we need to get first. We need a bike, and a nightlight, and one of those children parks. The kid is going to want a petting zoo. All kids love animals." Douglas barely glanced at her as he rushed after William. "William, wait, we need to talk about the petting zoo!"

Rachel slowly closed her mouth as the shock of their reaction wore off. Then, shaking her head, she stretched out on the couch and smiled. She touched her stomach, whispering, "Ah, little baby, I do love those two. You come from very strong roots and I'm going to tell you all about mine someday, starting with my Auntie Elvie and the best advice she ever gave me, 'let the wild out'."

The End

ABOUT THE AUTHOR

MICHELLE M. PILLOW WRITING AS MADELYN PORTER

New York Times & USA TODAY
Bestselling Author

Michelle loves to travel and try new things, whether it's a paranormal investigation of an old Vaudeville Theatre or climbing Mayan temples in Belize. She's addicted to movies and used to drive her mother crazy while quoting random scenes with her brother. Though it has yet to happen, her dream is to be a zombie in a horror movie. For the most part she can be found writing in her office with a cup of coffee while wearing pajama pants.

She loves to hear from readers. They can contact her through her website.

www.MichellePillow.com

facebook.com/AuthorMichellePillow

twitter.com/michellepillow

instagram.com/michellempillow

bookbub.com/authors/michelle-m-pillow

goodreads.com/Michelle_Pillow

amazon.com/author/michellepillow

youtube.com/michellepillow

pinterest.com/michellepillow

COMPLIMENTARY MATERIAL

BONUS CONTENT DOES NOT AFFECT THE
PRICE OF YOUR BOOK.

THE PLAYFUL PRINCE

BY MICHELLE M. PILLOW

The Playful Prince
Lords of the Var Series

Bestselling Shape-shifter Romance

To play...

Prince Quinn, royal Ambassador, isn't looking for a serious relationship. In fact, he's never even considered it. Hopping from lover to lover, he's content to enjoy himself, never taking anything but his work seriously. However, when Dr. Tori Elliot is sent to the palace to test for biological weapons, he can't seem to stay away from her.

Or not to play...

Tori Elliot has just finished her last assignment

and is on her way to a much needed vacation. But when the Human Intelligence Agency stops her ship and demands she heads up a team on some remote planet, she knows it in her best interest not to refuse. Ever serious, she knows she's there to do a job and no matter what, she's going to act like a professional.

Meeting Prince Quinn, his body pressed against another woman in the palace halls, she knows he's not the man for her. Too bad he's the Ambassador and too sexy for his own good. Fighting her desire, Tori must try to do her job while not succumbing to the playful Var prince.

The Playful Prince Excerpt

His sudden movement caught her attention and she realized he stepped toward her. He lifted his hand, as if to touch her. Tori flinched and took a step back.

"Sir," Tori stammered. "I mean, my ... ah?"

"Quinn," he supplied with a rakish smile.

"Yes, my Quinn... wait, no." She took another step back as he moved aggressively forward. The look on his face made her heart flutter in excitement.

"Your Quinn?" he mused in a low tone that sent chills over her spine. "You wish for me to be your Quinn?"

"Stop!" she demanded holding out her hand. He paused in his quest to get to her and grinned, waiting. Tori swallowed, nervous and distracted. "Prince Quinn. I am Dr. Elliot with ESC ... well, actually the HIA, well, not really, technically with HIA or ESC except—"

Was she babbling? Tori was pretty sure it sounded like she was babbling. Scientists didn't babble. It wasn't appropriate. Her scowl deepened. Oh, why was he continuing to look at her like that?

"Well, Dr. Elliot not technically with the HIA or ESC," Quinn said, lowering his jaw as he leaned forward. "I'm H O R N Y and you're extremely pretty."

"H O...? Oh! Really!" Tori gasped, dismayed. She shook her head in disapproval.

"What? You're really so surprised? Can you really blame me, Dr. Elliot? You were staring quite intently at—" Quinn began to motion down, acting as of their conversation was an everyday topic.

Tori held up her hand and shook her head frantically to stop him. Taking a deep breath, she centered her thoughts and made a silent promise to never drink the night before a big assignment again. Surely that is why her heart was pounding so hard and why her limbs were shaking. Swallowing, she forced her voice to rigid calmness. "Is there someone I could talk to about gaining permission to search the cave systems that the biological weapons were discovered in? The HIA has requested that I clear the cave and surrounding area of any and all contamination threats."

Someone other than you, she thought, not caring if he saw her distaste for his lewdness.

Quinn's smile faded and to her surprise, he turned serious. "You think something else is up there?"

"I'm honestly not sure. The recovered weapon appears to be intact and contains enough chemical to wipe out at least five planets. From that bit of information, I would assume there was only the one, unless the caves were being used as a storage unit of some kind, which, given the political climate of your Kingdom, doesn't seem to be the assumption. From what I understand, your father was fighting a war with..."

Tori stopped, realizing that she might be speaking too candidly. That's why she hated being in political situations. Facts were facts and she was use to stating them, regardless of their popularity. In her job facts were all that mattered. In politics, a person was supposed to say things diplomatically, twisting the words into just the right phrase. It was a skill she lacked. She looked up at the Prince. His face hadn't changed. She swallowed nervously. He motioned his hand slightly for her to continue, not looking at all offended by her words.

Weakly, Tori said, "My checking would simply be a wise safety precaution for everyone concerned, especially your people. It won't cost you a thing, if that's your concern. HIA is taking care of my and the other scientists' salary."

Quinn nodded, a motion she hoped was agreement.

"My team has nearly gotten through with the palace inhabitants and so far everyone has tested negative. I believe they're about finished." Tori looked at her clipboard and pretended to scan through the data. This man unnerved her. She couldn't concentrate on what she was saying to him. Was she repeating herself? Was he even listening? Did she tell him yet that they were about done testing the palace inhabitants? She thought it, but did she say it? Damn, he had the most brilliant blue eyes she'd ever seen in her life. Delicately clearing her throat, she said, "But, we'd still like to do a thorough scan of the caves. There is no point in us leaving anything behind."

Quinn seemed to contemplate her words. Tori lowered her voice and stepped closer. He didn't move, except for those blue eyes. They followed her, keeping fixed on her face.

Getting excited, Tori forgot her nervousness as she admitted in a secretive whisper, "There was also something else. I took the liberty of analyzing the strange dark mud on the biological weapon's crate. I believe it's from your marshes, because I found some fresh moss that leads me to believe it wasn't already on the crate when it was brought here. Anyway, there was an extremely high level of what appears to be DTH12 compound, which I'm sure isn't indigenous to this particular planet, being as your swamp soil is classified as GR13H and not TDH14. What doesn't make sense is that DTH12 is primarily found in the slime trail of northeastern yellow slugs on the planet of Fluk in the H ... what? Are you laughing at me?"

Quinn was indeed chuckling. Shaking his head, he said, "Woman, I have no idea what you just said."

Tori frowned. She should have known. Sarcastically, she drawled, "Your mud is neat and I'd like to look at it."

Okay, maybe that was a tad too condescending. Quinn grimaced but didn't appear overly offended. Lucky for her, because he might just be the man she had to impress.

For a complete, up-to-date booklist, visit
www.MichellePillow.com

PLEASE LEAVE A REVIEW

Please take a moment to share your thoughts by
scrolling to the end of the document to
rate/review this book.
Thank you for reading!

Please check out Madelyn's other titles at
www.MadelynPorter.com

Be sure to check out Michelle's other titles at
www.michellepillow.com